Academy Mystery Novellas

Volume 2
POLICE PROCEDURALS

Academy Mystery Novellas

Volume 2

POLICE PROCEDURALS

Edited by
Martin H. Greenberg & Bill Pronzini

Academy
Chicago
Publishers

Published in 1985 by

Academy Chicago Publishers
425 N. Michigan Ave.
Chicago, Illinois 60611

Printed and bound in the U.S.A.

Library of Congress Cataloging-in-Publication Data

Main entry under title:

Police procedurals.

     1. Police—Fiction.   2. Detective and mystery
stories, American.   I. Pronzini, Bill.   II. Greenberg,
Martin Harry.
PS374.P57P65   1985   813'.0872'08   85-18557
ISBN 0-89733-158-3

Academy Mystery Novellas are collections of long stories chosen on the basis of two criteria—(1) their excellence as mystery/suspense fiction and (2) their relative obscurity. This second criteria is due solely to the special limitations of the short novel/novella length—too short to be published alone as a novel but too long to be easily anthologized or collected, since they tend to take up too much space in a typical volume.

The series features long fiction by some of the best-known names in the crime fiction field, including such masters as Cornell Woolrich, Ed McBain, Georges Simenon, Donald E. Westlake, and many others. Each volume is organized around a type of crime story (locked-room, police procedural) or theme (type of detective, humor).

We are proud to bring these excellent works of fiction to your attention, and hope that you will enjoy reading them as much as we enjoyed the process of selecting them for you.

Martin H. Greenberg
Bill Pronzini

Contents

The Empty Hours
    Ed McBain 1

The Sound of Murder
    Donald E. Westlake 76

Storm in the Channel
    Georges Simenon 110

Murder in the Dark
    Hugh Pentecost 153

Notes about the Contributors 222

THE EMPTY HOURS
by Ed McBain

They thought she was colored at first.

The patrolman who investigated the complaint didn't expect to find a dead woman. This was the first time he'd seen a corpse, and he was somewhat shaken by the ludicrously relaxed grotesqueness of the girl lying on her back on the rug, and his hand trembled a little as he made out his report. But when he came to the blank line calling for an identification of RACE, he unhesitatingly wrote "Negro."

The call had been taken at Headquarters by a patrolman in the central Complaint Bureau. He sat at a desk with a pad of printed forms before him, and he copied down the information, shrugged because this seemed like a routine squeal, rolled the form and slipped it into a metal carrier, and then shot it by pneumatic tube to the radio room. A dispatcher there read the complaint form, shrugged because this seemed like a routine squeal, studied the precinct map on the wall opposite his desk, and then dispatched car eleven of the 87th Precinct to the scene.

The girl was dead.

She may have been a pretty girl, but she was hideous in death, distorted by the expanding gases inside her skin case. She was wearing a sweater and skirt, and she was barefoot, and her skirt had pulled back when she fell to the rug. Her head was twisted at a curious angle, the short black hair cradled by the rug, her eyes open and brown in a bloated face. The patrolman felt a sudden impulse to pull the girl's skirt down over her knees. He knew, suddenly, she would have wanted this. Death had caught her in this indecent posture, robbing her of female instinct. There were things this girl would never do again, so many things, all of which must have seemed enormously important to the girl herself. But the single universal thing was an infinitesimal detail, magnified now by death: she would never again perform the simple feminine and somehow beautiful act of pulling her skirt down over her knees.

The patrolman sighed and finished his report. The image of the dead girl remained in his mind all the way down to the squad car.

It was hot in the squadroom on that night in early August. The men working the graveyard shift had reported for duty at 6:00 P.M., and they would not go home until eight the following morning. They were all detectives and perhaps privileged members of the police force, but there were many policemen—Detective Meyer Meyer among them—who maintained that a uniformed cop's life made a hell of a lot more sense than a detective's.

"Sure, it does," Meyer insisted now, sitting at his desk in his shirt sleeves. "A patrolman's schedule provides regularity and security. It gives a man a home life."

"This squadroom is your home, Meyer," Carella said. "Admit it."

"Sure," Meyer answered, grinning. "I can't wait to come to work each day." He passed a hand over his bald pate. "You know what I like especially about this place? The interior decoration. The décor. It's very restful."

"Oh, you don't like your fellow workers, huh?" Carella said. He slid off the desk and winked at Cotton

Hawes, who was standing at one of the filing cabinets. Then he walked toward the water cooler at the other end of the room, just inside the slatted railing that divided squadroom from corridor. He moved with a nonchalant ease that was deceptive. Steve Carella had never been one of those weight-lifting goons, and the image he presented was hardly one of bulging muscular power. But there was a quiet strength about the man and the way he moved, a confidence in the way he casually accepted the capabilities and limitations of his body. He stopped at the water cooler, filled a paper cup, and turned to look at Meyer again.

"No, I like my colleagues," Meyer said. "In fact, Steve, if I had my choice in all the world of who to work with, I would choose you honorable, decent guys. Sure." Meyer nodded, building steam. "In fact, I'm thinking of having some medals cast off, so I can hand them out to you guys. Boy, am I lucky to have this job! I may come to work without pay from now on. I may just refuse my salary, this job is so enriching. I want to thank you guys. You make me recognize the real values in life."

"He makes a nice speech," Hawes said.

"He should run the line-up. It would break the monotony. How come you don't run the line-up, Meyer?"

"Steve, I been offered the job," Meyer said seriously. "I told them I'm needed right here at the Eighty-seventh, the garden spot of all the precincts. Why, they offered me chief of detectives, and when I said no, they offered me commissioner, but I was loyal to the squad."

"Let's give *him* a medal," Hawes said, and the telephone rang.

Meyer lifted the receiver. "Eighty-seventh Squad,

Detective Meyer. What? Yeah, just a second." He pulled a pad into place and began writing. "Yeah, I got it. Right. Right. Right. Okay." He hung up. Carella had walked to his desk. "A little colored girl," Meyer said.

"Yeah?"

"In a furnished room on South Eleventh."

"Yeah?"

"Dead," Meyer said.

II

The city doesn't seem to be itself in the very early hours of the morning.

She is a woman, of course, and time will never change that. She awakes as a woman, tentatively touching the day in a yawning, smiling stretch, her lips free of color, her hair tousled, warm from sleep, her body richer, an innocent girlish quality about her as sunlight stains the eastern sky and covers her with early heat. She dresses in furnished rooms in crumby rundown slums, and she dresses in Hall Avenue penthouses, and in the countless apartments that crowd the buildings of Isola and Riverhead and Calm's Point, in the private houses that line the streets of Bethtown and Majesta, and she emerges a different woman, sleek and businesslike, attractive but not sexy, a look of utter competence about her, manicured and polished, but with no time for nonsense, there is a long working day ahead of her. At five o'clock a metamorphosis takes place. She does not change her costume, this city, this woman, she wears the same frock or the same suit, the same high-heeled pumps or the same suburban loafers, but something breaks through that immaculate shell, a mood, a tone, an undercurrent. She is a different woman who sits in the bars and cocktail lounges, who relaxes on the patios or on the terraces shelving the skyscrapers, a different woman with a somewhat lazily inviting grin, a somewhat tired expression, an impenetrable knowledge on her face and in her eyes: she lifts her glass, she laughs gently, the evening sits expectantly on the skyline, the sky is awash with the purple of day's end.

She turns female in the night.

She drops her femininity and turns female. The polish is gone, the mechanized competence; she becomes a little scatterbrained and a little cuddly; she crosses her legs recklessly and allows her lipstick to be kissed clear off her mouth, and she responds to the male hands on her body, and she turns soft and inviting and miraculously primitive. The night is a female time, and the city is nothing but a woman.

And in the empty hours she sleeps, and she does not seem to be herself.

In the morning she will awake again and touch the silent air in a yawn, spreading her arms, the contented smile on her naked mouth. Her hair will be mussed, we will know her, we have seen her this way often.

But now she sleeps. She sleeps silently, this city. Oh, an eye open in the buildings of the night here and there, winking on, off again, silence. She rests. In sleep we do not recognize her. Her sleep is not like death, for we can hear and sense the murmur of life beneath the warm bedclothes. But she is a strange woman whom we have known intimately, loved passionately, and now she curls into an unresponsive ball beneath the sheet, and our hand is on her rich hip. We can feel life there, but we do not know her. She is faceless and featureless in the dark. She could be any city, any woman, anywhere. We touch her uncertainly. She has pulled the black nightgown of early morning around her. and we do not know her. She is a stranger, and her eyes are closed.

The landlady was frightened by the presence of policemen, even though she had summoned them. The taller one, the one who called himself Detective Hawes, was a redheaded giant with a white streak in his hair, a horror if she'd ever seen one. The landlady stood in the apartment where the girl lay dead on the rug, and she talked to the detectives in whispers, not because she was in the presence of death, but only because it was three o'clock in the morning. The landlady was wearing a bathrobe over her gown. There was an intimacy to the scene, the same intimacy that hangs alike over an impending fishing trip or a completed tragedy. Three A.M. is a time for slumber, and those who are awake while the city sleeps share a common bond that makes them friendly aliens.

"What's the girl's name?" Carella asked. It was three o'clock in the morning, and he had not shaved since five P.M. the day before, but his chin looked smooth. His eyes slanted slightly downward, combining with his clean-shaven face to give him a curiously oriental appearance. The landlady liked him. He was a nice boy, she thought. In her lexicon the men of the world were either "nice boys" or "louses." She wasn't sure about Cotton Hawes yet, but she imagined he was a parasitic insect.

"Claudia Davis," she answered, directing the answer to Carella whom she liked, and totally ignoring Hawes who had no right to be so big a man with a frightening white streak in his hair.

"Do you know how old she was?" Carella asked.

"Twenty-eight or twenty-nine, I think."

"Had she been living here long?"

"Since June," the landlady said.

"That short a time, huh?"

"And *this* has to happen," the landlady said. "She seemed like such a nice girl. Who do you suppose did it?"

"I don't know," Carella said.

"Or do you think it was suicide? I don't smell no gas, do you?"

"No," Carella said. "Do you know where she lived before this, Mrs. Mauder?"

"No, I don't."

"You didn't ask for references when she took the apartment?"

"It's only a furnished room," Mrs. Mauder said, shrugging. "She paid me a month's rent in advance."

"How much was that, Mrs. Mauder?"

"Sixty dollars. She paid it in cash. I never take checks from strangers."

"But you have no idea whether she's from this city, or out of town, or whatever. Am I right?"

"Yes, that's right."

"Davis," Hawes said, shaking his head. "That'll be a tough name to track down, Steve. Must be a thousand of them in the phone book."

"Why is your hair white?" the landlady asked.

"Huh?"

"That streak."

"Oh." Hawes unconsciously touched his left temple. "I got knifed once, he said, dismissing the question abruptly. "Mrs. Mauder, was the girl living alone?"

"I don't know. I mind my own business."

"Well, surely you would have seen . . ."

"I think she was living alone. I don't pry, and I don't spy. She gave me a month's rent in advance."

Hawes sighed. He could feel the woman's hostility. He decided to leave the questioning to Carella. "I'll take a look through the drawers and closets," he said, and moved off without waiting for Carella's answer.

"It's awfully hot in here," Carella said.

"The patrolman said we shouldn't touch anything until you got here," Mrs. Mauder said. "That's why I didn't open the windows or nothing."

"That was very thoughtful of you," Carella said, smiling. "But I think we can open the window now, don't you?"

"If you like. It does smell in here. Is . . . is that her? Smelling?"

"Yes," Carella answered. He pulled open the window. "There. That's a little better."

"Doesn't help much," the landlady said. "The weather's been terrible—just terrible. Body can't sleep at all." She looked down at the dead girl. "She looks just awful, don't she?"

"Yes. Mrs. Mauder, would you know where she worked, or if she had a job?"

"No, I'm sorry."

"Anyone ever come by asking for her? Friends? Relatives?"

"No, I'm sorry. I never saw any."

"Can you tell me anthing about her habits? When she left the house in the morning? When she returned at night?"

"I'm sorry; I never noticed."

"Well, what made you think something was wrong in here?"

"The milk. Outside the door. I was out with some

friends tonight, you see, and when I came back a man on the third floor called down to say his neighbor was playing the radio very loud and would I tell him to shut up, please. So I went upstairs and asked him to turn down the radio, and then I passed Miss Davis' apartment and saw the milk standing outside the door, and I thought this was kind of funny in such hot weather, but I figured it was *her* milk, you know, and I don't like to pry. So I came down and went to bed, but I couldn't stop thinking about that milk standing outside in the hallway. So I put on a robe and came upstairs and knocked on the door, and she didn't answer. So I called out to her, and she still didn't answer. So I figured something must be wrong. I don't know why. I just figured . . . I don't know. If she was in here, why didn't she answer?"

"How'd you know she was here?"

"I didn't."

"Was the door locked?"

"Yes."

"You tried it?"

"Yes. It was locked."

"I see," Carella said.

"Couple of cars just pulled up downstairs," Hawes said, walking over. "Probably the lab. And Homicide South."

"They know the squeal is ours," Carella said. "Why do they bother?"

"Make it look good," Hawes said. "Homicide's got the title on the door, so they figure they ought to go out and earn their salaries."

"Did you find anything?"

"A brand-new set of luggage in the closet, six pieces. The drawers and closets are full of clothes. Most of them look new. Lots of resort stuff, Steve. Found some brand-new books, too."

"What else?"

"Some mail on the dresser top."

"Anything we can use?"

Hawes shrugged. "A statement from the girl's bank. Bunch of canceled checks. Might help us."

"Maybe," Carella said. "Let's see what the lab comes up with."

The laboratory report came the next day, together with a necropsy report from the assistant medical examiner. In combination, the reports were fairly valuable. The first thing the detectives learned was that the girl was a white Caucasian of approximately thirty years of age.

Yes, white.

The news came as something of a surprise to the cops because the girl lying on the rug had certainly looked like a Negress. After all, her skin was black. Not tan, not coffee-colored, not brown, but black—that intensely black coloration found on primitive tribes who spend a good deal of their time in the sun. The conclusion seemed to be a logical one, but death is a great equalizer not without a whimsical humor all its own, and the funniest kind of joke is a sight gag. Death changes white to black, and when that grisly old man comes marching in there's no question of who's going to school with whom. There's no longer any question of pigmentation, friend. That girl on the floor looked black, but she was white, and whatever else she was she was also stone cold dead, and that's the worst you can do to anybody.

The report explained that the girl's body was in a state of advanced putrefaction, and it went into such esoteric terms as "general distention of the body cavities, tissues, and blood vessels with gas," and "black discoloration of the skin, mucous membranes, and irides caused by hemolysis and action of hydrogen sulfide on the blood pigment," all of which broke down to the simple fact that it was a damn hot week in August and the girl had been lying on a rug which retained heat and speeded the post-mortem putrefaction. From what they could tell, and in weather like this, it was mostly a guess, the girl had been dead and decomposing for at least forty-eight hours, which set the time of her demise as August first or thereabouts.

One of the reports went on to say that the clothes she'd been wearing had been purchased in one of the city's larger department stores. All of her clothes—those she wore and those found in her apartment—were rather expensive, but someone at the lab thought it necessary to note that all her panties were trimmed with Belgian lace and retailed for twenty-five dollars a pair. Someone else at the lab mentioned that a thorough examination of her garments and her body had revealed no traces of blood, semen, or oil stains.

The coroner fixed the cause of death as strangulation.

III

It is amazing how much an apartment can sometimes yield to science. It is equally amazing, and more than a little disappointing, to get nothing from the scene of a murder when you are desperately seeking a clue. The furnished room in which Claudia Davis had been strangled to death was full of juicy surfaces conceivably carrying hundreds of latent fingerprints. The closets and drawers contained piles of clothing that might have carried traces of anything from gunpowder to face powder.

But the lab boys went around lifting their prints and sifting their dust and vacuuming with a Söderman-Heuberger filter, and they went down to the morgue and studied the girl's skin and came up with a total of nothing. Zero. Oh, not quite zero. They got a lot of prints belonging to Claudia Davis, and a lot of dust collected from all over the city and clinging to her shoes and her furniture. They also found some documents belonging to the dead girl—a birth certificate, a diploma of graduation from a high school in Santa Monica, and an expired library card. And, oh, yes, a key. The key didn't seem to fit any of the locks in the room. They sent all the junk over to the 87th, and Sam Grossman called Carella personally later that day to apologize for the lack of results.

The squadroom was hot and noisy when Carella took the call from the lab. The conversation was a curiously one-sided affair. Carella, who had dumped the contents of the laboratory envelope onto his desk, merely grunted or nodded every now and then. He thanked Grossman at last, hung up, and stared at the window facing the street and Grover Park.

"Get anything?" Meyer asked.

"Yeah. Grossman thinks the killer was wearing gloves."

"That's nice," Meyer said.

"Also, I think I know what this key is for." He lifted it from the desk.

"Yeah? What?"

"Well, did you see these canceled checks?"

"No."

"Take a look," Carella said.

He opened the brown bank envelope addressed to Claudia Davis, spread the canceled checks on his desk top, and then unfolded the yellow bank statement. Meyer studied the display silently.

"Cotton found the envelope in her room," Carella said. "The statement covers the month of July. Those are all the checks she wrote, or at least everything that cleared the bank by the thirty-first."

"Lots of checks here," Meyer said.

"Twenty-five, to be exact. What do you think?"

"I know what *I* think," Carella said.

"What's that?"

"I look at those checks, I can see a life. It's like reading somebody's diary. Everything she did last month is right here, Meyer. All the department stores she went to, look, a florist, her hairdresser, a candy shop, even her shoemaker, and look at this. A check made out to a funeral home. Now who died, Meyer, huh? And look here. She was living at Mrs. Mauder's place, but here's a check made out to a swank apartment building on the South Side, in Stewart City. And some of these checks are just made out to names, *people*. This case is crying for some people."

"You want me to get the phone book?"

"No, wait a minute. Look at this bank statement. She opened the account on July fifth with a thousand bucks. All of a sudden, bam, she deposits a thousand bucks in the Seaboard Bank of America."

"What's so odd about that?"

"Nothing, maybe. But Cotton called the other banks in the city, and Claudia Davis has a very healthy account at the Highland Trust on Cromwell Avenue. And I mean *very* healthy."

"How healthy?"

"Close to sixty grand."

"What!"

"You heard me. And the Highland Trust lists no withdrawals for the month of July. So where'd she get the money to put into Seaboard?"

"Was that the only deposit?"

"Take a look."

Meyer picked up the statement.

"The initial deposit was on July fifth," Carella said. "A thousand bucks. She made another thousand-dollar deposit on July twelfth. And another on the nineteenth. And another on the twenty-seventh."

Meyer raised his eyebrows. "Four grand. That's a lot of loot."

"And all deposited in less than a month's time. I've got to work almost a full year to make that kind of money."

"Not to mention the sixty grand in the other bank. Where do you suppose she got it, Steve?"

"I don't know. It just doesn't make sense. She wears underpants trimmed with Belgian lace, but she lives in a crumby room-and-a-half with bath. How the hell do you figure that? Two bank accounts, twenty-five bucks to cover her ass, and all she pays is sixty bucks a month for a flophouse."

"Maybe she's hot, Steve."

"No." Carella shook his head. "I ran a make with C.B.I. She hasn't got a record, and she's not wanted for anything. I haven't heard from the feds yet, but I imagine it'll be the same story."

"What about that key? You said . . ."

"Oh, yeah. That's pretty simple, thank God. Look at this."

He reached into the pile of checks and sorted out a yellow slip, larger than the checks. He handed it to Meyer. The slip read:

THE SEABOARD BANK OF AMERICA
Isola Branch
P 1698

_____July 5_____

We are charging your account as per items below. Please see that the amount is deducted on your books so that our accounts may agree.

FOR			
Safe deposit rental #375		5	00
U.S. Tax			50
AMOUNT OF CHARGE		5	50

CHARGE___ Claudia Davis

1263 South Eleventh

Isola

ENTERED BY

BPR

"She rented a safe-deposit box the same day she opened the new checking account, huh?" Meyer said.

"Right."

"What's in it?"

"That's a good question."

"Look, do you want to save some time, Steve?"

"Sure."

"Let's get the court order *before* we go to the bank."

The manager of the Seaboard Bank of America was a bald-headed man in his early fifties. Working on the theory that similar physical types are *simpático*, Carella allowed Meyer to do most of the questioning. It was not easy to elicit answers from Mr. Anderson, the manager of the bank, because he was by nature a reticent man. But Detective Meyer Meyer was the most patient man in the city, if not the entire world. His patience was an acquired trait, rather than an inherited one. Oh, he had inherited a few things from his father, a jovial man named Max Meyer, but patience was not one of them. If anything, Max Meyer had been a very impatient if not downright short-tempered sort of fellow. When his wife, for example, came to him with the news that she was expecting a baby, Max nearly hit the ceiling. He enjoyed little jokes immensely, was perhaps the biggest practical joker in all Riverhead, but this particular prank of nature failed to amuse him. He had thought his wife was long past the age when bearing children was even a remote possibility. He never thought of himself as approaching dotage, but he was after all getting on in years, and a change-of-life baby was hardly what the doctor had ordered. He allowed the impending birth to simmer inside him, planning his revenge all the while, plotting the practical joke to end all practical jokes.

When the baby was born, he named it Meyer, a delightful handle which when coupled with the family name provided the infant with a double-barreled monicker: Meyer Meyer.

Now that's pretty funny. Admit it. You can split your sides laughing over that one, unless you happen to be a pretty sensitive kid who also happens to be an Orthodox Jew, and who happens to live in a predominately Gentile neighborhood. The kids in the neighborhood thought Meyer Meyer had been invented solely for their own pleasure. If they needed further provocation for beating up the Jew boy, and they didn't need any, his name provided excellent motivational fuel. "Meyer, Meyer, Jew on fire!" they would shout, and then they would chase him down the street and beat hell out of him.

Meyer learned patience. It is not very often that one kid, or even one grown man, can successfully defend himself against a gang. But sometimes you can talk yourself out of a beating. Sometimes, if you're patient, if you just wait long enough, you can catch one of them alone and stand up to him face to face, man to man, and know the exultation of a fair fight without the frustration of overwhelming odds.

Listen, Max Meyer's joke was a harmless one. You can't deny an old man his pleasure. But Mr. Anderson, the manager of the bank, was fifty-four years old and totally bald. Meyer Meyer, the detective second grade who sat opposite him and asked questions, was also totally bald. Maybe a lifetime of sublimation, a lifetime of devoted patience, doesn't leave any scars. Maybe not. But Meyer Meyer was only thirty-seven years old.

Patiently he said, "Didn't you find these large deposits rather odd, Mr. Anderson?"

"No," Anderson said. "A thousand dollars is not a lot of money."

"Mr. Anderson," Meyer said patiently, "you are aware, of course, that banks in this city are required to report to the police any unusually large sums of money deposited at one time. You are aware of that, are you not?"

"Yes, I am."

"Miss Davis deposited four thousand dollars in three weeks' time. Didn't that seem unusual to you?"

"No. The deposits were spaced. A thousand dollars is not a lot of money, and not an unusually large deposit."

"To me," Meyer said, "a thousand dollars is a lot of money. You can buy a lot of beer with a thousand dollars."

"I don't drink beer," Anderson said flatly.

"Neither do I," Meyer answered.

"Besides, we *do* call the police whenever we get a very large deposit, unless the depositor is one of our regular customers. I did not feel these deposits warranted such a call."

"Thank you, Mr. Anderson," Meyer said. "We have a court order here. We'd like to open the box Miss Davis rented."

"May I see the order, please?" Anderson said. Meyer showed it to him. Anderson sighed and said, "Very well. Do you have Miss Davis' key?"

Carella reached into his pocket. "Would this be it?" he said. He put a key on the desk. It was the key that had come to him from the lab together with the documents they'd found in the apartment.

"Yes, that's it," Mr. Anderson said. "There are two different keys to every box, you see. The bank keeps one, and the renter keeps the other. The box cannot be opened without both keys. Will you come with me, please?"

He collected the bank key to safety-deposit box number 375 and led the detectives to the rear of the bank. The room seemed to be lined with shining metal. The boxes, row upon row, reminded Carella of the morgue and the refrigerated shelves that slid in and out of the wall on squeaking rollers. Anderson pushed the bank key into a slot and turned it, and then he put Claudia Davis' key into a second slot and turned that. He pulled the long, thin box out of the wall and handed it to Meyer. Meyer carried it to the counter on the opposite wall and lifted the catch.

"Okay?" he said to Carella.

"Go ahead."

Meyer raised the lid of the box.

There was $16,000 in the box. There was also a slip of note paper. The $16,000 was neatly divided into four stacks of bills. Three of the stacks held $5,000 each. The fourth stack held only $1,000. Carella picked up the slip of paper. Someone, presumably Claudia Davis, had made some annotations on it in pencil.

$$
\begin{array}{ll}
7/5 & 20,000 \\
7/5 & -1,000 \\
\hline
& 19,000 \\
7/12 & -1,000 \\
\hline
& 18,000 \\
7/19 & -1,000 \\
\hline
& 17,000 \\
7/27 & -1,000 \\
\hline
& 16,000 \\
\end{array}
$$

"Make any sense to you, Mr. Anderson?"

"No, I'm afraid not."

"She came into this bank on July fifth with twenty thousand dollars in cash, Mr. Anderson. She put a thousand of that into a checking account and the remainder into this box. The dates on this slip of paper show exactly when she took cash from the box and transferred it to the checking account. She knew the rules, Mr. Anderson. She knew that twenty grand deposited in one lump would bring a call to the police. This way was a lot safer."

"We'd better get a list of these serial numbers," Meyer said.

"Would you have one of your people do that for us, Mr. Anderson?"

Anderson seemed ready to protest. Instead, he looked at Carella, sighed, and said, "Of course."

The serial numbers didn't help them at all. They compared them against their own lists, and the out-of-town lists, and the FBI lists, but none of those bills was hot.

Only August was.

V

Stewart City hangs in the hair of Isola like a jeweled tiara. Not really a city, not even a town, merely a collection of swank apartment buildings overlooking the River Dix, the community had been named after British royalty and remained one of the most exclusive neighborhoods in town. If you could boast of a Stewart City address, you could also boast of a high income, a country place on Sands Spit, and a Mercedes Benz in the garage under the apartment building. You could give your address with a measure of snobbery and pride—you were, after all, one of the elite.

The dead girl named Claudia Davis had made out a check to Management Enterprises, Inc., at 13 Stewart Place South, to the tune of $750. The check had been dated July ninth, four days after she'd opened the Seaboard account.

A cool breeze was blowing in off the river as Carella and Hawes pulled up. Late-afternoon sunlight dappled the polluted water of the Dix. The bridges connecting Calm's Point with Isola hung against a sky awaiting the assault of dusk.

"Want to pull down the sun visor?" Carella said.

Hawes reached up and turned down the visor. Clipped to the visor so that it showed through the windshield of the car was a hand-lettered card that read POLICEMAN ON DUTY CALL—87TH PRECINCT. The car, a

1956 Chevrolet, was Carella's own.

"I've got to make a sign for my car," Hawes said. "Some bastard tagged it last week."

"What did you do?"

"I went to court and pleaded not guilty. On my day off."

"Did you get out of it?"

"Sure. I was answering a squeal. It's bad enough I had to use my own car, but for Pete's sake, to get a ticket!"

"I prefer my own car," Carella said. "Those three cars belonging to the squad are ready for the junk heap."

"*Two*," Hawes corrected. "One of them's been in the police garage for a month now."

"Meyer went down to see about it the other day."

"What'd they say? Was it ready?"

"No, the mechanic told him there were four patrol cars ahead of the sedan, and they took precedence. Now how about that?"

"Sure, it figures. I've still got a chit in for the gas I used, you know that?"

"Forget it. I've never got back a cent I laid out for gas."

"What'd Meyer do about the car?"

"He slipped the mechanic five bucks. Maybe that'll speed him up."

"You know what the city ought to do?" Hawes said. "They ought to buy some of those used taxicabs. Pick them up for two or three hundred bucks, paint them over, and give them out to the squads. Some of them are still in pretty good condition."

"Well, it's an idea," Carella said dubiously, and they entered the building. They found Mrs. Miller, the manager, in an office at the rear of the ornate entrance lobby. She was a woman in her early forties with a well-preserved figure and a very husky voice. She wore her hair piled on the top of her head, a pencil stuck rakishly into the reddish-brown heap. She looked at the photo-stated check and said, "Oh, yes, of course."

"You knew Miss Davis?"

"Yes, she lived here for a long time."

"How long?"

"Five years."

"When did she move out?"

"At the end of June." Mrs. Miller crossed her splen-did legs and smiled graciously. The legs were remarkable for a woman of her age, and the smile was almost radiant. She moved with an expert femininity, a calcu-lated conscious fluidity of flesh that suggested availability and yet was totally respectable. She seemed to have de-voted a lifetime to learning the ways and wiles of the female and now practiced them with facility and charm. She was pleasant to be with, this woman, pleasant to watch and to hear, and to think of touching. Carella and Hawes, charmed to their shoes, found themselves relax-ing in her presence.

"This check," Carella said, tapping the photostat. "What was it for?"

"June's rent. I received it on the tenth of July. Claudia always paid her rent by the tenth of the month. She was a very good tenant."

"The apartment cost seven hundred and fifty dollars a month?"

"Yes."

"Isn't that high for an apartment?"

"Not in Stewart City," Mrs. Miller said gently. "And this was a river-front apartment."

"I see. I take it Miss Davis had a good job."

"No, no, she doesn't have a job at all."

"Then how could she afford . . . ?"

"Well, she's rather well off, you know."

"Where does she get the money, Mrs. Miller?"

"Well . . ." Mrs. Miller shrugged. "I really think you should ask *her*, don't you? I mean, if this is something concerning Claudia, shouldn't you . . . ?"

"Mrs. Miller," Carella said, "Claudia Davis is dead."

"What?"

"She's . . ."

"What? No. No." She shook her head. "Claudia? But the check . . . I . . . the check came only last month." She shook her head again. "No. No."

"She's dead, Mrs. Miller," Carella said gently. "She was strangled."

The charm faltered for just an instant. Revulsion knifed the eyes of Mrs. Miller, the eyelids flickered, it seemed for an instant that the pupils would turn shining and wet, that the carefully lipsticked mouth would crumble. And then something inside took over, something that demanded control, something that reminded her that a charming woman does not weep and cause her fashionable eye make-up to run.

"I'm sorry," she said, almost in a whisper. "I am really, really sorry. She was a nice person."

"Can you tell us what you know about her, Mrs. Miller?"

"Yes. Yes, of course." She shook her head again, unwilling to accept the idea. "That's terrible. That's terrible. Why, she was only a baby."

"We figured her for thirty, Mrs. Miller. Are we wrong?"

"She seemed younger, but perhaps that was because . . . well, she was a rather shy person. Even when she first came here, there was an air of—well, lostness about her. Of course, that was right after her parents died, so . . ."

"Where did she come from, Mrs. Miller?"

"California. Santa Monica."

Carella nodded. "You were starting to tell us . . . you said she was rather well off. Could you . . . ?"

"Well, the stock, you know."

"What stock?"

"Her parents had set up a securities trust account for her. When they died, Claudia began receiving the income from the stock. She was an only child, you know."

"And she lived on stock dividends alone?"

"They amounted to quite a bit. Which she saved, I might add. She was a very systematic person, not at all frivolous. When she received a dividend check, she would endorse it and take it straight to the bank. Claudia was a very sensible girl."

"Which bank, Mrs. Miller?"

"The Highland Trust. Right down the street. On Cromwell Avenue."

"I see," Carella said. "Was she dating many men? Would you know?"

"I don't think so. She kept pretty much to herself. Even after Josie came."

Carella leaned forward. "Josie? Who's Josie?"

"Josie Thompson. Josephine, actually. Her cousin."

"And where did *she* come from?"

"California. They both came from California."

"And how can we get in touch with this Josie Thompson?"

"Well, she... Don't you know? Haven't you...?"

"What, Mrs. Miller?"

"Why, Josie is dead. Josie passed on in June. That's why Claudia moved, I suppose. I suppose she couldn't bear the thought of living in that apartment without Josie. It *is* a little frightening, isn't it?"

"Yes," Carella said.

DETECTIVE DIVISION SUPPLEMENTARY REPORT	SQUAD	PRECINCT	PRECINCT REPORT	DETECTIVE DIVISION REPORT NUMBER
pdcn 360 rev 25m	87	87	32-101	DD 60 R-42

NAME AND ADDRESS OF PERSON REPORTING	DATE ORIGINAL REPORT
Miller Irene (Mrs. John) 13 Stewart Place S.	8-4-60
SURNAME GIVEN NAME INITIALS NUMBER STREET	

Summary of interview with Irene (Mrs. John)
Miller at office of Management Enterrpises, Inc.,
address above, in re homicide Claudia Davis.
Mrs. Miller states:

Claudia Davis came to this city in June of
1955, took $750-a-month apartment above address,
lived there alone. Rarely seen in company of
friends, male or female. Young recluse type
living on substantial income of inehrited
securities. Parents, Mr. and Mrs. Carter Davis,
killed on San Diego Freeway in headon collision
with station wagon, April 14, 1955. L.A.P.D. con-
firms traffic accident, driver of other vehicle
convicted for negligent operation. Mrs. Miller
describes girl as medium height and weight,
close-cropped brunette hair, brown eyes, no scars
or birthmarks she can remember, tallies with what
we have on corpse. Further says Claudia Davis was
quiet, unobtrusive tenant, paid rent and all
service bills punctually; was gentle, sweet,
plain, childlike, shy, meticulous in money
matters, well liked but unapproachable.

In April or May of 1959, Josie
Thompson, cousin of deceased, arrived from Brent-
wood, California. (Routine check with Criminal
Bureau Identification negarive, no record. Checking now with L.A.P.D., and F.B.I.). Described as
slightly older than Claudia, rather different in
looks and personality. "They were like black and
white," Mrs. Miller says, "but they hit it off
exceptionally well." Josie moved into the apartment with cousin. Words used to describe rela-
tionship between two were "like the closest

sisters" and "really in tune" and "the best of
friends," etc. Girls did not date much, were
constantly in each other's company, Josie seeming
to pick up recluse habits from Claudia. Went on
frequent trips together. Spent summer of '59 on
Tortoise Island in the bay, returned Labor Day.
Went away again at Christmas time to ski Sun
Valley, and again in March this year to Kingston,
Jamaica, for three weeks, returning at beginning
of April. Source of income was fairly standard
securities-income account. Claudia did not own
the stock, but income on it was hers for as long
as she lived. Trust specified that upon her death
the stock and the income be turned over to
U.C.L.A. (father's alma mater). In any case,
Claudia was assured of a very, very substantial
lifetime income (see Highland Trust bank account)
and was apparently supporting Josie as well,
since Mrs. Miller claims neither girl worked.
Brought up question of possible lesbianism, but
Mrs. Miller, who is knowledgeable and hip, says
no, neither girl was a dike.

On June 3, Josie and Claudia left for
another weekend trip. Dorrman reports having
helped them packed valises into trunk of Claudia's
car, 1960 Cadillac convertible. Claudia did the
driving. Girls did not return on Monday morning
as they had indicated they would. Claudia called
on Wednesday, crying on telephone. Told Mrs.
Miller that Josie had had a terrible accident and
was dead. Mrs. Miller remembers asking Claudia if
she could help in any way. Claudia said, quote,
No, everything's been taken care of already,
unquote.

On June 17, Mrs. Miller received a letter
from Claudia (letter attached - hadnwriting com-
pares positive with checks Claudia signed) stating she could not possibly return to apartment,
not after what had happened to her cousin. She
reminded Mrs. Miller lease expired on July 4,
told her she would send check for June's rent
before July 10. Said moving company would pack
and pick up her belongings, delivering all valu-
ables and documents to her, and storing rest.
(See Claudia Davis' check number 010, 7/14,
made payable to Allora Brothers, Inc., "in payment for packing, moving, and storage.") Claudia

Davis never returned to the apartment. Mrs.
Miller had not seen her and knew nothing of her
whereabouts until we informed her of the
homicide.

DATE OF THIS REPORT				
August 6				

Det 2/gr Carella S.L.		714-56-32	Det/Lt. Peter Byrnes
RANK SURNAME INITIALS		SHIELD NUMBER	COMMANDING OFFICER

VI

The drive upstate to Triangle Lake was a particularly scenic one, and since it was August, and since Sunday was supposed to be Carella's day off, he thought he might just as well combine a little business with pleasure. So he put the top of the car down, and he packed Teddy into the front seat together with a picnic lunch and a gallon Thermos of iced coffee, and he forgot all about Claudia Davis on the drive up through the mountains. Carella found it easy to forget about almost anything when he was with his wife.

Teddy as far as he was concerned—and his astute judgment had been backed up by many a street-corner whistle—was only the most beautiful woman in the world. He could never understand how he, a hairy, corny, ugly, stupid, clumsy cop, had managed to capture anyone as wonderful as Theodora Franklin. But capture her he had, and he sat beside her now in the open car and stole sidelong glances at her as he drove, excited as always by her very presence.

Her black hair, always wild, seemed to capture something of the wind's frenzy as it whipped about the oval of her face. Her brown eyes were partially squinted against the rush of air over the windshield. She wore a white blouse emphatically curved over a full bosom, black tapered slacks form-fitted over generous hips and good legs. She had kicked off her sandals and folded her knees against her breasts, her bare feet pressed against the glove-compartment panel. There was about her, Carella realized, a curious combination of savage and sophisticate. You never knew whether she was going to kiss you or slug you, and the uncertainty kept her eternally desirable and exciting.

Teddy watched her husband as he drove, his big-knuckled hands on the wheel of the car. She watched him not only because it gave her pleasure to watch him, but also because he was speaking. And since she could not hear, since she had been born a deaf mute, it was essential that she look at his mouth when he spoke. He did not discuss the case at all. She knew that one of the Claudia Davis checks had been made out to the Fancher Funeral Home in Triangle Lake and she knew that Carella wanted to talk to the proprietor of the place personally. She further knew that this was very important or he wouldn't be spending his Sunday driving all the way upstate. But he had promised her he'd combine business with pleasure. This was the pleasure part of the trip, and in deference to his promise and his wife, he refrained from discussing the case, which was really foremost in his mind. He talked, instead, about the scenery, and their plans for the fall, and the way the twins were growing, and how pretty Teddy looked, and how she'd better button that top button of her blouse before they got out of the car, but he never once mentioned Claudia Davis until they were standing in the office of the Fancher Funeral Home and looking into the gloomy eyes of a man who called himself Barton Scoles.

Scoles was tall and thin and he wore a black suit that he had probably worn to his own confirmation back in 1912. He was so much the stereotype of a small-town undertaker that Carella almost burst out laughing when he met him. Somehow, though, the environment was not conducive to hilarity. There was a strange smell hovering over the thick rugs and the papered walls and the hanging chandeliers. It was a while before Carella recognized it as formaldehyde and then made the automatic association and, curious for a man who had stared into the eyes of death so often, suddenly felt like retching.

"Miss Davis made out a check to you on July fifteenth," Carella said. "Can you tell me what it was for?"

"Sure can," Scoles said. "Had to wait a long time for that check. She give me only a twenty-five dollar deposit. Usually take fifty, you know. I got stuck many a time, believe me."

"How do you mean?" Carella asked.

"People. You bury their dead, and then sometimes they don't pay you for your work. This business isn't *all* fun, you know. Many's the time I handled the whole funeral and the service and the burial and all, and never did get paid. Makes you lose your faith in human nature."

"But Miss Davis finally *did* pay you."

"Oh, sure. But I can tell you I was sweating that one out. I can tell you that. After all, she was a strange gal from the city, has the funeral here, nobody comes to it but her, sitting in the chapel out there and watching the body as if someone's going to steal it away, just her and the departed. I tell you, Mr. Carella . . . Is that your name?"

"Yes, Carella."

"I tell you, it was kind of spooky. Lay there two days, she did, her cousin. And then Miss Davis asked that we bury the girl right here in the local cemetery, so I done that for her, too—all on the strength of a twenty-five dollar deposit. That's trust, Mr. Carella, with a capital T."

"When was this, Mr. Scoles?"

"The girl drowned the first weekend in June," Scoles said. "Had no business being out on the lake so early, anyways. That water's still icy cold in June. Don't really warm up none till the latter part July. She fell over the side of the boat—she was out there rowing, you know—and that icy water probably froze her solid, or give her cramps or something, drowned her anyways." Scoles shook his head. "Had no business being out on the lake so early."

"Did you see a death certificate?"

"Yep, Dr. Donneli made it out. Cause of death was drowning, all right, no question about it. We had an inquest, too, you know. The Tuesday after she drowned. They said it was accidental."

"You said she was out rowing in a boat. Alone?"

"Yep. Her cousin, Miss Davis, was on the shore watching. Jumped in when she fell overboard, tried to reach her, but couldn't make it in time. That water's plenty cold, believe me. Ain't too warm even now, and here it is August already."

"But it didn't seem to affect Miss Davis, did it?"

"Well, she was probably a strong swimmer. Been my experience most pretty girls are strong girls, too. I'll bet your wife here is a strong girl. She sure is a pretty one."

Scoles smiled, and Teddy smiled and squeezed Carella's hand.

"About the payment," Carella said, "for the funeral and the burial. Do you have any idea why it took Miss Davis so long to send her check?"

"Nope. I wrote her twice. First time was just a friendly little reminder. Second time, I made it a little stronger. Attorney friend of mine in town wrote it on his stationery; that always impresses them. Didn't get an answer either time. Finally, right out of the blue, the check came, payment in full. Beats me. Maybe she was affected by the death. Or maybe she's always slow paying her debts. I'm just happy the check came, that's all. Sometimes the live ones can give you more trouble than them who's dead, believe me."

They strolled down to the lake together, Carella and his wife, and ate their picnic lunch on its shores. Carella was strangely silent. Teddy dangled her bare feet in the water. The water, as Scoles had promised, was very cold even though it was August. On the way back from the lake Carella said, "Honey, would you mind if I make one more stop?"

Teddy turned her eyes to him inquisitively.

"I want to see the chief of police here."

Teddy frowned. The question was in her eyes, and he answered it immediately.

"To find out whether or not there were any witnesses to that drowning. *Besides* Claudia Davis, I mean. From the way Scoles was talking, I get the impression that lake was pretty deserted in June."

The chief of police was a short man with a pot belly and big feet. He kept his feet propped up on his desk all the while he spoke to Carella. Carella watched him and wondered why everybody in the damn town seemed to be on vacation from an MGM movie. A row of rifles in a locked rack was behind the chief's desk. A host of WANTED fliers covered a bulletin board to the right of the rack. The chief had a hole in the sole of his left shoe.

"Yep," he said, "there was a witness, all right."

Carella felt a pang of disappointment. "Who?" he asked.

"Fellow fishing at the lake. Saw the whole thing. Testified before the coroner's jury."

"What'd he say?"

"Said he was fishing there when Josie Thompson took the boat out. Said Claudia Davis stayed behind, on the shore. Said Miss Thompson fell overboard and went under like a stone. Said Miss Davis jumped in the water and began swimming toward her. Didn't make it in time. That's what he said."

"What else did he say?"

"Well, he drove Miss Davis back to town in her car. 1960 Caddy convertible, I believe. She could hardly speak. She was sobbing and mumbling and wringing her hands, oh, in a hell of a mess. Why, we had to get the whole story out of that fishing fellow. Wasn't until the next day that Miss Davis could make any kind of sense."

"When did you hold the inquest?"

"Tuesday. Day before they buried the cousin. Coroner did the dissection on Monday. We got authorization from Miss Davis, Penal Law 2213, next of kin being charged by law with the duty of burial may authorize dissection for the sole purpose of ascertaining the cause of death."

"And the coroner reported the cause of death as drowning?"

"That's right. Said so right before the jury."

"Why'd you have an inquest? Did you suspect something more than accidental drowning?"

"Not necessarily. But that fellow who was fishing, well, *he* was from the city, too, you know. And for all we knew him and Miss Davis could have been in this together, you know, shoved the cousin over the side of the boat, and then faked up a whole story, you know. They both coulda been lying in their teeth."

"Were they?"

"Not so we could tell. You never seen anybody so grief-stricken as Miss Davis was when the fishing fellow drove her into town. Girl would have to be a hell of an actress to behave that way. Calmed down the next day, but you shoulda seen her when it happened. And at the inquest it was plain this fishing fellow had never met her before that day at the lake. Convinced the jury he had no prior knowledge of or connection with either of the two girls. Convinced me, too, for that matter."

"What's his name?" Carella asked. "This fishing fellow."

"Courtenoy."

"What did you say?"

"Courtenoy. Sidney Courtenoy."

"Thanks," Carella answered, and he rose suddenly. "Come on, Teddy. I want to get back to the city."

VII

Courtenoy lived in a one-family clapboard house in Riverhead. He was rolling up the door of his garage when Carella and Meyer pulled into his driveway early Monday morning. He turned to look at the car curiously, one hand on the rising garage door. The door stopped, halfway up, halfway down. Carella stepped into the driveway.

"Mr. Courtenoy?" he asked.

"Yes?" He stared at Carella, puzzlement on his face, the puzzlement that is always there when a perfect stranger addresses you by name. Courtenoy was a man in his late forties, wearing a cap and a badly fitted sports jacket and dark flannel slacks in the month of August. His hair was graying at the temples. He looked tired, very tired, and his weariness had nothing whatever to do with the fact that it was only seven o'clock in the morning. A lunch box was at his feet where he had apparently put it when he began rolling up the garage door. The car in the garage was a 1953 Ford.

"We're police officers," Carella said. "Mind if we ask you a few questions?"

"I'd like to see your badge," Courtenoy said. Carella showed it to him. Courtenoy nodded as if he had performed a precautionary public duty. "What are your questions?" he said. "I'm on my way to work. Is this about that damn building permit again?"

"What building permit?"

"For extending the garage. I'm buying my son a little jalopy, don't want to leave it out on the street. Been having a hell of a time getting a building permit. Can you imagine that? All I want to do is add another twelve feet to the garage. You'd think I was trying to build a city park or something. Is that what this is about?"

From inside the house a woman's voice called, "Who is it, Sid?"

"Nothing, nothing," Courtenoy said impatiently. "Nobody. Never mind, Bett." He looked at Carella. "My wife. You married?"

"Yes, sir, I'm married," Carella said.

"Then you know," Courtenoy said cryptically. "What are your questions?"

"Ever see this before?" Carella asked. He handed a photostated copy of the check to Courtenoy, who looked at it briefly and handed it back.

"Sure."

"Want to explain it, Mr. Courtenoy?"

"Explain what?"

"Explain why Claudia Davis sent you a check for a hundred and twenty dollars."

"As recompense," Courtenoy said unhesitatingly.

"Oh, recompense, huh?" Meyer said. "For what, Mr. Courtenoy? For a little cock-and-bull story?"

"Huh? What are you talking about?"

"Recompense for *what*, Mr. Courtenoy?"

"For missing three days' work, what the hell did you think?"

"How's that again?"

"No, what did you *think*?" Courtenoy said angrily, waving his finger at Meyer. "What did you think it was for? Some kind of payoff or something? Is that what you thought?"

"Mr. Courtenoy . . ."

"I lost three days' work because of that damn inquest. I had to stay up at Triangle Lake all day Monday and Tuesday and then again on Wednesday waiting for the jury decision. I'm a bricklayer. I get five bucks an hour and I lost three days' work, eight hours a day, and so Miss Davis was good enough to send me a check for a hundred and twenty bucks. Now just what the hell did you think, would you mind telling me?"

"Did you know Miss Davis before that day at Triangle Lake, Mr. Courtenoy?"

"Never saw her before in my life. What is this? Am I on trial here? What is this?"

From inside the house the woman's voice came again, sharply, "Sidney! Is something wrong? Are you all right?"

"Nothing's wrong. Shut up, will you?"

There was an aggrieved silence from within the clapboard structure. Courtenoy muttered something under his breath and then turned to face the detectives again. "You finished?" he said.

"Not quite, Mr. Courtenoy. We'd like you to tell us what you saw that day at the lake."

"What the hell for? Go read the minutes of the inquest if you're so damn interested. I've got to get to work."

"That can wait, Mr. Courtenoy."

"Like hell it can. This job is away over in . . ."

"Mr. Courtenoy, we don't want to have to go all the way downtown and come back with a warrant for your arrest."

"My *arrest!* For what? Listen, what did I . . .?"

"Sidney? Sidney, shall I call the police?" the woman shouted from inside the house.

"Oh, shut the hell up!" Courtenoy answered. "Call the police," he mumbled. "I'm up to my ears in cops, and she wants to call the police. What do you want from me? I'm an honest bricklayer. I saw a girl drown. I told it just the way I saw it. Is that a crime? Why are you bothering me?"

"Just tell it again, Mr. Courtenoy. Just the way you saw it."

"She was out in the boat," Courtenoy said, sighing. "I was fishing. Her cousin was on the shore. She fell over the side."

"Josie Thompson."

"Yes, Josie Thompson, whatever the hell her name was."

"She was alone in the boat?"

"Yes. She was alone in the boat."

"Go on."

"The other one—Miss Davis—screamed and ran into the water, and began swimming toward her." He shook his head. "She didn't make it in time. That boat was a long way out. When she got there, the lake was still. She dove under and came up, and then dove under again, but it was too late, it was just too late. Then, as she was swimming back, I thought *she* was going to drown, too. She faltered and sank below the surface, and I waited and I thought sure she was gone. Then there was a patch of yellow that broke through the water, and I saw she was all right."

"Why didn't you jump in to help her, Mr. Courtenoy?"

"I don't know how to swim."

"All right. What happened next?"

"She came out of the water—Miss Davis. She was exhausted and hysterical. I tried to calm her down, but she kept yelling and crying, not making any sense at all. I dragged her over to the car, and I asked her for the car keys. She didn't seem to know what I was talking about at first. 'The keys!' I said, and she just stared at me. 'Your car keys!' I yelled. 'The keys to the car.' Finally she reached in her purse and handed me the keys."

"Go on."

"I drove her into town. It was me who told the story to the police. She couldn't talk, all she could do was babble and scream and cry. It was a terrible thing to watch. I'd never before seen a woman so completely off her nut. We couldn't get two straight words out of her until the next day. Then she was all right. Told the police who she was, explained what I'd already told them the day before, and told them the dead girl was her cousin, Josie Thompson. They dragged the lake and got her out of the water. A shame. A real shame. Nice young girl like that."

"What was the dead girl wearing?"

"Cotton dress. Loafers, I think. Or sandals. Little thin sweater over the dress. A cardigan."

"Any jewelry?"

"I don't think so. No."

"Was she carrying a purse?"

"No. Her purse was in the car with Miss Davis'."

"What was Miss Davis wearing?"

"When? The day of the drowning? Or when they pulled her cousin out of the lake?"

"Was she there then?"

"Sure. Identified the body."

"No, I wanted to know what she was wearing on the day of the accident, Mr. Courtenoy."

"Oh, a skirt and a blouse, I think. Ribbon in her hair. Loafers. I'm not sure."

"What color blouse? Yellow?"

"No. Blue."

"You said yellow."

"No, blue. I didn't say yellow."

Carella frowned. "I thought you said yellow earlier." He shrugged. "All right, what happened after the inquest?"

"Nothing much. Miss Davis thanked me for being so kind and said she would send me a check for the time I'd missed. I refused at first and then I thought, What the hell, I'm a hard-working man, and money doesn't grow on trees. So I gave her my address. I figured she could afford it. Driving a Caddy, and hiring a fellow to take it back to the city."

"Why didn't she drive it back herself?"

"I don't know. I guess she was still a little shaken. Listen, that was a terrible experience. Did you ever see anyone die up close?"

"Yes," Carella said.

From inside the house Courtenoy's wife yelled, "Sidney, tell those men to get out of our driveway!"

"You heard her," Courtenoy said, and finished rolling up his garage door.

VIII

Nobody likes Monday morning.

It was invented for hang-overs. It is really not the beginning of a new week, but only the tail end of the week before. Nobody likes it, and it doesn't have to be rainy or gloomy or blue in order to provoke disaffection. It can be bright and sunny and the beginning of August. It can start with a driveway interview at seven A.M. and grow progressively worse by nine-thirty that same morning. Monday is Monday and legislature will never change its personality. Monday is Monday, and it stinks.

By nine-thirty that Monday morning, Detective Steve Carella was on the edge of total bewilderment and, like any normal person, he blamed it on Monday. He had come back to the squadroom and painstakingly gone over the pile of checks Claudia Davis had written during the month of July, a total of twenty-five, searching them for some clue to her strangulation, studying them with the scrutiny of a typographer in a print shop. Several things seemed evident from the checks, but nothing seemed pertinent. He could recall having said: "I look at those checks, I can see a life. It's like reading somebody's diary," and he was beginning to believe he had uttered some famous last words in those two succinct sentences. For if this was the diary of Claudia Davis, it was a singularly unprovocative account that would never make the nation's best-seller lists.

Most of the checks had been made out to clothing or department stores. Claudia, true to the species, seemed to have a penchant for shopping and a checkbook that yielded to her spending urge. Calls to the various stores represented revealed that her taste ranged through a wide variety of items. A check of sales slips showed that she had purchased during the month of July alone three baby doll nightgowns, two half slips, a trenchcoat, a wrist watch, four pairs of tapered slacks in various colors, two pairs of walking shoes, a pair of sunglasses, four Bikini swimsuits, eight wash-and-wear frocks, two skirts, two cashmere sweaters, half-a-dozen best-selling novels, a large bottle of aspirin, two bottles of Dramamine, six pieces of luggage, and four boxes of cleansing tissue. The most expensive thing she had purchased was an evening gown costing $500. These purchases accounted for most of the checks she had drawn in July. There were also checks to a hairdresser, a florist, a shoemaker, a candy shop, and three unexplained checks that were drawn to individuals, two men and a woman.

The first was made out to George Badueck.

The second was made out to David Oblinsky.

The third was made out to Martha Fedelson.

Someone on the squad had attacked the telephone directory and come up with addresses for two of the three. The third, Oblinsky, had an unlisted number, but a half-hour's argument with a supervisor had finally netted an address for him. The completed list was now on Carella's desk together with all the canceled checks. He should have begun tracking down those names, he knew, but something still was bugging him.

"Why did Courtenoy lie to me and Meyer?" he asked Cotton Hawes. "Why did he lie about something as simple as what Claudia Davis was wearing on the day of the drowning?"

"How did he lie?"

"First he said she was wearing yellow, said he saw a patch of yellow break the surface of the lake. Then he changed it to blue. Why did he do that, Cotton?"

"I don't know."

"And if he lied about that, why couldn't he and Claudia have done in little Josie together?"

"I don't know," Hawes said.

"Where'd that twenty thousand bucks come from, Cotton?"

"Maybe it was a stock dividend."

"Maybe. Then why didn't she simply deposit the check? This was cash, Cotton, *cash*. Now where did it come from? That's a nice piece of change. You don't pick twenty grand out of the gutter."

"I suppose not."

"I know where you can get twenty grand, Cotton."

"Where?"

"From an insurance company. When someone dies." Carella nodded once, sharply. "I'm going to make some calls. Damnit, that money had to come from *someplace*."

He hit pay dirt on his sixth call. The man he spoke to was named Jeremiah Dodd and was a representative of the Security Insurance Corporation, Inc. He recognized Josie Thompson's name at once.

"Oh, yes," he said. "We settled that claim in July."

"Who made the claim, Mr. Dodd?"

"The beneficiary, of course. Just a moment. Let me get the folder on this. Will you hold on, please?"

Carella waited impatiently. Over at the insurance company on the other end of the line he could hear muted voices. A girl giggled suddenly, and he wondered who was kissing whom over by the water cooler. At last Dodd came back on the line.

"Here it is," he said. "Josephine Thompson. Beneficiary was her cousin, Miss Claudia Davis. Oh, yes, now it's all coming back. Yes, this is the one."

"What one?"

"Where the girls were mutual beneficiaries."

"What do you mean?"

"The cousins," Dodd said. "There were two life policies. One for Miss Davis and one for Miss Thompson. And they were mutual beneficiaries."

"You mean Miss Davis was the beneficiary of Miss Thompson's policy and vice versa?"

"Yes, that's right."

"That's very interesting. How large were the policies?"

"Oh, very small."

"Well, how *small* then?"

"I believe they were both insured for twelve thousand five hundred. Just a moment; let me check. Yes, that's right."

"And Miss Davis applied for payment on the policy after her cousin died, huh?"

"Yes. Here it is, right here. Josephine Thompson drowned at Lake Triangle on June fourth. That's right. Claudia Davis sent in the policy and the certificate of death and also a coroner's jury verdict."

"She didn't miss a trick, did she?"

"Sir? I'm sorry, I . . ."

"Did you pay her?"

"Yes. It was a perfectly legitimate claim. We began processing it at once."

"Did you send anyone up to Lake Triangle to investigate the circumstances of Miss Thompson's death?"

"Yes, but it was merely a routine investigation. A coroner's inquest is good enough for us, Detective Carella."

"When did you pay Miss Davis?"

"On July first."

"You sent her a check for twelve thousand five

hundred dollars, is that right?"

"No, sir."

"Didn't you say . . . ?"

"The policy insured her for twelve-five, that's correct. But there was a double-indemnity clause, you see, and Josephine Thompson's death was accidental. No, we had to pay the policy's limit, Detective Carella. On July first we sent Claudia Davis a check for twenty-five thousand dollars."

IX

There are no mysteries in police work.

Nothing fits into a carefully preconceived scheme. The high point of any given case is very often the corpse that opens the case. There is no climactic progression; suspense is for the movies. There are only people and curiously twisted motives, and small unexplained details, and coincidence, and the unexpected, and they combine to form a sequence of events, but there is no real mystery, there never is. There is only life, and sometimes death, and neither follows a rule book. Policemen hate mystery stories because they recognize in them a control that is lacking in their own very real, sometimes routine, sometimes spectacular, sometimes tedious investigation of a case. It is very nice and very clever and very convenient to have all the pieces fit together neatly. It is very kind to think of detectives as master mathematicians working on an algebraic problem whose constants are death and a victim, whose unknown is a murderer. But many of these mastermind detectives have trouble adding up the deductions on their twice-monthly pay checks.

The world is full of wizards, for sure, but hardly any of them work for the city police.

There was one big mathematical discrepancy in the Claudia Davis case.

There seemed to be $5,000 unaccounted for.

Twenty-five grand had been mailed to Claudia Davis on July 1, and she presumably received the check after the Fourth of July holiday, cashed it someplace, and then took her money to the Seaboard Bank of America, opened a new checking account, and rented a safety-deposit box. But her total deposit at Seaboard had been $20,000 whereas the check had been for $25,000, so where was the laggard five? And who had cashed the check for her? Mr. Dodd of the Security Insurance Corporation, Inc., explained the company's rather complicated accounting system to Carella. A check was kept in the local office for several days after it was cashed in order to close out the policy, after which it was sent to the main office in Chicago where it sometimes stayed for several weeks until the master files were closed out. It was then sent to the company's accounting and auditing firm in San Francisco. It was Dodd's guess that the canceled check had already been sent to the California accountants, and he promised to put a tracer on it at once. Carella asked him to please hurry. Someone had cashed that check for Claudia and, supposedly, someone also had one fifth of the check's face value.

The very fact that Claudia had not taken the check itself to Seaboard seemed to indicate that she had something to hide. Presumably, she did not want anyone asking questions about insurance company checks, or insurance policies, or double indemnities, or accidental drownings, or especially her cousin Josie. The check was a perfectly good one, and yet she had chosen to cash it *before* opening a new account. Why? And why, for that matter, had she bothered opening a new account when she had a rather well-stuffed and active account at another bank?

There are only whys in police work, but they do not add up to mystery. They add up to work, and nobody in the world likes work. The bulls of the 87th would have preferred to sit on their backsides and sip at gin-and-tonics, but the whys were there, so they put on their hats and their holsters and tried to find some becauses.

Cotton Hawes systematically interrogated each and every tenant in the rooming house where Claudia Davis had been killed. They all had alibis tighter than the closed fist of an Arabian stablekeeper. In his report to the lieutenant, Hawes expressed the belief that none of the tenants was guilty of homicide. As far as he was concerned, they were all clean.

Meyer Meyer attacked the 87th's stool pigeons. There were money-changers galore in the precinct and the city, men who turned hot loot into cold cash—for a price. If someone had cashed a $25,000 check for Claudia and kept $5,000 of it during the process, couldn't that person conceivably be one of the money-changers? He put the precinct stoolies on the ear, asked them to sound around for word of a Security Insurance Corporation check. The stoolies came up with nothing.

Detective Lieutenant Sam Grossman took his laboratory boys to the murder room and went over it again. And again. And again. He reported that the lock on the door was a snap lock, the kind that clicks shut automatically when the door is slammed. Whoever killed Claudia Davis could have done so without performing any locked-room gymnastics. All he had to do was close the door behind him when he left. Grossman also reported that Claudia's bed had apparently not been slept in on the night of the murder. A pair of shoes had been found at the foot of a large easy chair in the bedroom and a novel was wedged open on the arm of the chair. He suggested that Claudia had fallen asleep while reading, had awakened, and gone into the other room where she had met her murderer and her death. He had no suggestions as to just who that murderer might have been.

Steve Carella was hot and impatient and overloaded. There were other things happening in the precinct, things like burglaries and muggings and knifings and assaults and kids with summertime on their hands hitting other kids with ball bats because they didn't like the way they pronounced the word "*señor.*" There were telephones jangling, and reports to be typed in triplicate, and people filing into the squadroom day and night with complaints against the citizenry of that fair city, and the Claudia Davis case was beginning to be a big fat pain in the keester. Carella wondered what it was like to be a shoemaker. And while he was wondering, he began to chase down the checks made out to George Badueck, David Oblinsky, and Martha Fedelson.

Happily, Bert Kling had nothing whatsoever to do with the Claudia Davis case. He hadn't even discussed it with any of the men on the squad. He was a young detective and a new detective, and the things that happened in that precinct were enough to drive a guy nuts and keep him busy forty-eight hours every day, so he didn't go around sticking his nose into other people's cases. He had enough troubles of his own. One of those troubles was the line-up.

On Wednesday morning Bert Kling's name appeared on the line-up duty chart.

X

The line-up was held in the gym downtown at Headquarters on High Street. It was held four days a week, Monday to Thursday, and the purpose of the parade was to acquaint the city's detectives with the people who were committing crime, the premise being that crime is a repetitive profession and that a crook will always be a crook, and it's good to know who your adversaries are should you happen to come face to face with them on the street. Timely recognition of a thief had helped crack many a case and had, on some occasions, even saved a detective's life. So the line-up was a pretty valuable in-group custom. This didn't mean that detectives enjoyed the trip downtown. They drew line-up perhaps once every two weeks and, often as not, line-up duty fell on their day off, and nobody appreciated rubbing elbows with criminals on his day off.

The line-up that Wednesday morning followed the classic pattern of all line-ups. The detectives sat in the gymnasium on folding chairs, and the chief of detectives sat behind a high podium at the back of the gym. The green shades were drawn, and the stage illuminated, and the offenders who'd been arrested the day before were marched before the assembled bulls while the chief read off the charges and handled the interrogation. The pattern was a simple one. The arresting officer, uniformed or plain-clothes, would join the chief at the rear of the gym when his arrest came up. The chief would read off the felon's name, and then the section of the city in which he'd been arrested, and then a number. He would say, for example, "Jones, John, Riverhead, three." The "three" would simply indicate that this was the third arrest in Riverhead that day. Only felonies and special types of misdemeanors were handled at the line-up, so this narrowed the list of performers on any given day. Following the case number, the chief would read off the offense, and then say either "Statement" or "No statement," telling the assembled cops that the thief either had or had not said anything when they'd put the collar on him. If there had been a statement, the chief would limit his questions to rather general topics since he didn't want to lead the felon into saying anything that might contradict his usually incriminating initial statement, words that could be used against him in court. If there had been *no* statement, the chief would pull out all the stops. He was generally armed with whatever police records were available on the man who stood under the blinding lights, and it was the smart thief who understood the purpose of the line-up and who knew he was not bound to answer a goddamned thing they asked him. The chief of detectives was something like a deadly earnest Mike Wallace, but the stakes were slightly higher here because this involved something a little more important than a novelist plugging his new book or a senator explaining the stand he had taken on a farm bill. These were truly "interviews in depth," and the booby prize was very often a long stretch up the river in a cozy one-windowed room.

The line-up bored the hell out of Kling. It always did. It was like seeing a stage show for the hundredth time. Every now and then somebody stopped the show with a really good routine. But usually it was the same old song and dance. It wasn't any different that Wednesday. By the time the eighth offender had been paraded and subjected to the chief's bludgeoning interrogation, Kling was beginning to doze. The detective sitting next to him nudged him gently in the ribs.

". . . Reynolds, Ralph," the chief was saying, "Isola, four. Caught burgling an apartment on North Third. No statement. How about it, Ralph?"

"How about what?"

"You do this sort of thing often?"

"What sort of thing?"

"Burglary."

"I'm no burglar," Reynolds said.

"I've got his B-sheet here," the chief said. "Arrested for burglary in 1948, witness withdrew her testimony, claimed she had mistakenly identified him. Arrested again for burglary in 1952, convicted for Burglary One, sentenced to ten at Castleview, paroled in '58 on good behavior. You're back at the old stand, huh, Ralph?"

"No, not me. I've been straight ever since I got out."

"Then what were you doing in that apartment during the middle of the night?"

"I was a little drunk. I must have walked into the wrong building."

"What do you mean?"

"I thought it was my apartment."

"Where do you live, Ralph?"

"On . . . uh . . . well . . ."

"Come on, Ralph."

"Well, I live on South Fifth."

"And the apartment you were in last night is on North Third. You must have been pretty drunk to wander that far off course."

"Yeah, I guess I was pretty drunk."

"Woman in that apartment said you hit her when she woke up. Is that true, Ralph?"

"No. No, hey, I never hit her."

"She says so, Ralph."

"Well, she's mistaken."

"Well, now, a doctor's report says somebody clipped

her on the jaw, Ralph, now how about that?"

"Well, maybe."

"Yes or no?"

"Well, maybe when she started screaming she got me nervous. I mean, you know, I thought it was my apartment and all."

"Ralph, you were burgling that apartment. How about telling us the truth?"

"No, I got in there by mistake."

"How'd you get in?"

"The door was open."

"In the middle of the night, huh? The door was open?"

"Yeah."

"You sure you didn't pick the lock or something, huh?"

"No, no. Why would I do that? I thought it was my apartment."

"Ralph, what were you doing with burglar's tools?"

"Who? Who me? Those weren't burglar's tools."

"Then what were they? You had a glass cutter, and a bunch of jimmies, and some punches, and a drill and bits, and three celluloid strips, and some lock-picking tools, and eight skeleton keys. Those sound like burglar's tools to me, Ralph."

"No. I'm a carpenter."

"Yeah, you're a carpenter all right, Ralph. We searched your apartment, Ralph, and found a couple of things we're curious about. Do you always keep sixteen wrist watches and four typewriters and twelve bracelets and eight rings and a mink stole and three sets of silverware, Ralph?"

"Yeah. I'm a collector."

"Of other people's things. We also found four hundred dollars in American currency and five thousand dollars in French francs. Where'd you get that money, Ralph?"

"Which?"

"Whichever you feel like telling us about."

"Well, the U.S. stuff I . . . I won at the track. And the other, well, a Frenchman owed me some gold, and so he paid me in francs. That's all."

"We're checking our stolen-goods list right this minute, Ralph."

"So check!" Reynolds said, suddenly angry. "What the hell do you want from me? Work for your goddamn living! You want it all on a platter! Like fun! I told you everything I'm gonna . . ."

"Get him out of here," the chief said. "Next, Blake, Donald, Bethtown, two. Attempted rape. No statement . . ."

Bert Kling made himself comfortable on the folding chair and began to doze again.

XI

The check made out to George Badueck was numbered 018. It was a small check, five dollars. It did not seem very important to Carella, but it was one of the unexplained three, and he decided to give it a whirl.

Badueck, as it turned out, was a photographer. His shop was directly across the street from the County Court Building in Isola. A sign in his window advised that he took photographs for chauffeurs' licenses, hunting licenses, passports, taxicab permits, pistol permits, and the like. The shop was small and crowded. Badueck fitted into the shop like a beetle in an ant trap. He was a huge man with thick, unruly black hair and the smell of developing fluid on him.

"Who remembers?" he said. "I get millions of people in here every day of the week. They pay me in cash, they pay me with checks, they're ugly, they're pretty, they're skinny, they're fat, they all look the same on the pictures I take. Lousy. They all look like I'm photographing them for you guys. You never see any of these official-type pictures? Man, they look like mug shots, all of them. So who remembers this . . . what's her name? Claudia Davis, yeah. Another face that's all. Another mug shot. Why? Is the check bad or something?"

"No, it's a good check."

"So what's the fuss?"

"No fuss," Carella said. "Thanks a lot."

He sighed and went out into the August heat. The County Court Building across the street was white and Gothic in the sunshine. He wiped a handkerchief across his forehead and thought, *Another face, that's all.* Sighing, he crossed the street and entered the building. It was cool in the high vaulted corridors. He consulted the directory and went up to the Bureau of Motor Vehicles first. He asked the clerk there if anyone named Claudia Davis had applied for a license requiring a photograph.

"We only require pictures on chauffeurs' licenses," the clerk said.

"Well, would you check?" Carella asked.

"Sure. Might take a few minutes, though. Would you have a seat?"

Carella sat. It was very cool. It felt like October. He looked at his watch. It was almost time for lunch, and he was getting hungry. The clerk came back and motioned him over.

"We've got a Claudia Davis listed," he said, "but she's already got a license, and she didn't apply for a new one."

"What kind of license?"

"Operator's"

"When does it expire?"

"Next September."

"And she hasn't applied for anything needing a photo?"

"Nope. Sorry."

"That's all right. Thanks," Carella said.

He went out into the corridor again. He hardly thought it likely that Claudia Davis had applied for a permit to own or operate a taxicab, so he skipped the Hack Bureau and went upstairs to Pistol Permits. The woman he spoke to there was very kind and very efficient. She checked her files and told him that no one named Claudia Davis had ever applied for either a carry or a premises pistol permit. Carella thanked her and went into the hall again. He was very hungry. His stomach was beginning to growl. He debated having lunch and then returning and decided, *Hell, I'd better get it done now.*

The man behind the counter in the Passport Bureau was old and thin and he wore a green eyeshade. Carella asked his question, and the old man went to his files and creakingly returned to the window.

"That's right," he said.

"What's right?"

"She did. Claudia Davis. She applied for a passport."

"When?"

The old man checked the slip of paper in his trembling hands. "July twentieth," he said.

"Did you give it to her?"

"We accepted her application, sure. Isn't us who issues the passports. We've got to send the application on to Washington."

"But you did accept it?"

"Sure, why not? Had all the necessary stuff. Why shouldn't we accept it?"

"What was the necessary stuff?"

"Two photos, proof of citizenship, filled-out application, and cash."

"What did she show as proof of citizenship?"

"Her birth certificate."

"Where was she born?"

"California."

"She paid you in cash?"

"That's right."

"Not a check?"

"Nope. She started to write a check, but the blamed pen was on the blink. We use ballpoints, you know, and it gave out after she filled in the application. So she paid me in cash. It's not all that much money, you know."

"I see. Thank you," Carella said.

"Not at all," the old man replied, and he creaked back to his files to replace the record on Claudia Davis.

The check was numbered 007, and it was dated July twelfth, and it was made out to a woman named Martha Fedelson.

Miss Fedelson adjusted her pince-nez and looked at the check. Then she moved some papers aside on the small desk in the cluttered office, and put the check down, and leaned closer to it, and studied it again.

"Yes," she said, "that check was made out to me. Claudia Davis wrote it right in this office." Miss Fedelson smiled. "If you can call it an office. Desk space and a telephone. But then, I'm just starting, you know."

"How long have you been a travel agent, Miss Fedelson?"

"Six months now. It's very exciting work."

"Had you ever booked a trip for Miss Davis before?"

"No. This was the first time."

"Did someone refer her to you?"

"No. She picked my name out of the phone book."

"And asked you to arrange this trip for her, is that right?"

"Yes."

"And this check? What's it for?"

"Her airline tickets, and deposits at several hotels."

"Hotels *where?*"

"In Paris and Dijon. And then another in Lausanne, Switzerland."

"She was going to Europe?"

"Yes. From Lausanne she was heading down to the Italian Riviera. I was working on that for her, too. Getting transportation and the hotels, you know."

"When did she plan to leave?"

"September first."

"Well, that explains the luggage and the clothes," Carella said aloud.

"I'm sorry," Miss Fedelson said, and she smiled and raised her eyebrows.

"Nothing, nothing," Carella said. "What was your impression of Miss Davis?"

"Oh, that's hard to say. She was only here once, you understand." Miss Fedelson thought for a moment, and then said, "I suppose she *could* have been a pretty girl if she tried, but she wasn't trying. Her hair was short and dark, and she seemed rather—well, withdrawn, I guess. She didn't take her sunglasses off all the while she was here. I suppose you would call her shy. Or frightened. I don't know." Miss Fedelson smiled again. "Have I helped you any?"

"Well, now we know she was going abroad," Carella said.

"September is a good time to go," Miss Fedelson an-

swered. "In September the tourists have all gone home."
There was a wistful sound to her voice. Carella thanked
her for her time and left the small office with its travel
folders on the cluttered desk top.

XII

He was running out of checks and running out of
ideas. Everything seemed to point toward a girl in flight,
a girl in hiding, but what was there to hide, what was
there to run from? Josie Thompson had been in that boat
alone. The coroner's jury had labeled it accidental drowning. The insurance company hadn't contested Claudia's
claim, and they'd given her a legitimate check that she
could have cashed anywhere in the world. And yet there
was hiding, and there *was* flight—and he couldn't understand why.

He took the list of remaining checks from his
pocket. The girl's shoemaker, the girl's hairdresser, a
florist, a candy shop. None of them truly important.
And the remaining check made out to an individual, the
check numbered 006 and dated July eleventh, and written to a man named David Oblinsky in the amount of
$45.75. Carella had his lunch at two-thirty and then went
downtown. He found Oblinsky in a diner near the bus
terminal. Oblinsky was sitting on one of the counter
stools, and he was drinking a cup of coffee. He asked
Carella to join him, and Carella did.

"You traced me through that check, huh?" he said.
"The phone company gave you my number and my address, huh? I'm unlisted, you know. They ain't supposed
to give out my number."

"Well, they made a special concession because it was
police business."

"Yeah, well, suppose the cops called and asked for Marlon Brando's number? You think they'd give it out? Like hell they would. I don't like that. No, sir, I don't like it one damn bit."

"What do you do, Mr. Oblinsky? Is there a reason for the unlisted number?"

"I drive a cab is what I do. Sure there's a reason. It's classy to have an unlisted number. Didn't you know that?"

Carella smiled. "No, I didn't."

"Sure, it is."

"Why did Claudia Davis give you this check?" Carella asked.

"Well, I work for a cab company here in this city, you see. But usually on weekends or on my day off I use my own car and I take people on long trips, you know what I mean? Like to the country, or the mountains, or the beach, wherever they want to go."

"I see."

"Sure. So in June sometime, the beginning of June it was, I get a call from this guy I know up at Triangle Lake, he tells me there's a rich broad there who needs somebody to drive her Caddy back to the city for her. He said it was worth thirty bucks if I was willing to take the train up and the heap back. I told him, no sir, I wanted forty-five or it was no deal. I knew I had him over a barrel, you understand? He'd already told me he checked with the local hicks and none of them felt like making the ride. So he said he would talk it over with her and get back to me. Well, he called again . . . you know, it burns me up about the phone company. They ain't supposed to give out my number like that. Suppose it was Marilyn Monroe? You think they'd give out her number? I'm gonna raise a stink about this, believe me."

"What happened when he called you back?"

"Well, he said she was willing to pay forty-five, but

like could I wait until July sometime when she would send me a check because she was a little short right at the moment. So I figured what the hell, am I going to get stiffed by a dame who's driving a 1960 Caddy? I figured I could trust her until July. But I also told him, if that was the case, then I also wanted her to pay the tolls on the way back, which I don't ordinarily ask my customers to do. That's what the seventy-five cents was for. The tolls."

"So you took the train up there and then drove Miss Davis and the Cadillac back to the city, is that right?"

"Yeah."

"I suppose she was pretty distraught on the trip home."

"Huh?"

"You know. Not too coherent."

"Huh?"

"Broken up. Crying. Hysterical," Carella said.

"No. No, she was okay."

"Well, what I mean is . . ." Carella hesitated. "I assumed she wasn't capable of driving the car back herself."

"Yeah, that's right. That's why she hired me."

"Well, then . . ."

"But not because she was broken up or anything."

"Then why?" Carella frowned. "Was there a lot of luggage? Did she need your help with that?"

"Yeah, sure. Both hers and her cousin's. Her cousin drowned, you know."

"Yes. I know that."

"But anybody coulda helped her with the luggage," Oblinsky said. "No, that wasn't why she hired me. She really *needed* me, mister."

"Why?"

"Why? Because she don't know how to drive, that's why."

Carella stared at him. "You're wrong," he said.

"Oh, no," Oblinsky said. "She can't drive, believe me. While I was putting the luggage in the trunk, I asked her to start the car, and she didn't even know how to do that. Hey, you think I ought to raise a fuss with the phone company?"

"I don't know," Carella said, rising suddenly. All at once the check made out to Claudia Davis' hairdresser seemed terribly important to him. He had almost run out of checks, but all at once he had an idea.

XIII

The hairdresser's salon was on South Twenty-third, just off Jefferson Avenue. A green canopy covered the sidewalk outside the salon. The words ARTURO MAN-FREDI, INC., were lettered discreetly in white on the canopy. A glass plaque in the window repeated the name of the establishment and added, for the benefit of those who did not read either *Vogue* or *Harper's Bazaar*, that there were two branches of the shop, one here in Isola and another in "Nassau, the Bahamas." Beneath that, in smaller more modest letters, were the words "Internationally Renowned." Carella and Hawes went into the shop at four-thirty in the afternoon. Two meticulously coifed and manicured women were sitting in the small reception room, their expensively sleek legs crossed, apparently awaiting either their chauffeurs, their husbands, or their lovers. They both looked up expectantly when the detectives entered, expressed mild disappointment by only slightly raising newly plucked eyebrows, and went back to reading their fashion magazines. Carella and Hawes walked to the desk. The girl behind the desk was a blonde with a brilliant shellacked look and an English finishing school voice.

"Yes?" she said. "May I help you?"

She lost a tiny trace of her poise when Carella flashed his buzzer. She read the raised lettering on the shield, glanced at the photo on the plastic-encased I.D. card, quickly regained her polished calm, and said coolly and unemotionally, "Yes, what can I do for you?"

"We wonder if you can tell us anything about the girl who wrote this check?" Carella said. He reached into his jacket pocket, took out a folded photostat of the check, unfolded it, and put it on the desk before the blonde. The blonde looked at it casually.

"What is the name?" she asked. "I can't make it out."

"Claudia Davis."

"D-A-V-I-S?"

"Yes."

"I don't recognize the name," the blonde said. "She's not one of our regular customers."

"But she did make a check to your salon," Carella said. "She wrote this on July seventh. Would you please check your records and find out why she was here and who took care of her?"

"I'm sorry," the blonde said.

"What?"

"I'm sorry, but we close at five o'clock, and this is the busiest time of the day for us. I'm sure you can understand that. If you'd care to come back a little later . . ."

"No, we wouldn't care to come back a little later," Carella said. "Because if we came back a little later, it would be with a search warrant and possibly a warrant for the seizure of your books, and sometimes that can cause a little commotion among the gossip columnists, and that kind of commotion might add to your international renown a little bit. We've had a long day, miss, and this is important, so how about it?"

"Of course. We're always delighted to cooperate with the police," the blonde said frigidly. "Especially when they're so well mannered."

"Yes, we're all of that," Carella answered.

"Yes. July seventh, did you say?"

"July seventh."

The blonde left the desk and went into the back of the salon. A brunette came out front and said, "Has Miss Marie left for the evening?"

"Who's Miss Marie?" Hawes asked.

"The blonde girl."

"No. She's getting something for us."

"That white streak is very attractive," the brunette said. "I'm Miss Olga."

"How do you do."

"Fine, thank you," Miss Olga said. "When she comes back, would you tell her there's something wrong with one of the dryers on the third floor?"

"Yes, I will," Hawes said.

Miss Olga smiled, waved, and vanished into the rear of the salon again. Miss Marie reappeared not a moment later. She looked at Carella and said, "A Miss Claudia Davis was here on July seventh. Mr. Sam worked on her. Would you like to talk to him?"

"Yes, we would."

"Then follow me, please," she said curtly.

They followed her into the back of the salon past women who sat with crossed legs, wearing smocks, their heads in hair dryers.

"Oh, by the way," Hawes said, "Miss Olga said to tell you there's something wrong with one of the third-floor dryers."

"Thank you," Miss Marie said.

Hawes felt particularly clumsy in this world of women's machines. There was an air of delicate efficiency about the place, and Hawes—six feet two inches tall in his bare soles, weighing in at a hundred and ninety pounds—was certain he would knock over a bottle of nail polish or a pail of hair rinse. As they entered the second-floor salon, as he looked down that long line of humming space helmets at women with crossed legs and what looked like barbers' aprons covering their nylon slips, he became aware of a new phenomenon. The women were slowly turning their heads inside the dryers to look at the white streak over his left temple. He suddenly felt like a horse's ass. For whereas the streak was the legitimate result of a knifing—they had shaved his red hair to get at the wound, and it had grown back this way—he realized all at once that many of these women had shelled out hard-earned dollars to simulate identical white streaks in their own hair, and he no longer felt like a cop making a business call. Instead, he felt like a customer who had come to have his goddamned streak touched up a little.

"This is Mr. Sam," Miss Marie said, and Hawes turned to see Carella shaking hands with a rather elongated man. The man wasn't particularly tall, he was simply elongated. He gave the impression of being seen from the side seats in a movie theater, stretched out of true proportion, curiously two-dimensional. He wore a white smock, and there were three narrow combs in the breast pocket. He carried a pair of scissors in one thin, sensitive-looking hand.

"How do you do?" he said to Carella, and he executed a half-bow, European in origin, American in execution. He turned to Hawes, took his hand, shook it, and again said, "How do you do?"

"They're from the police," Miss Marie said briskly,

releasing Mr. Sam from any obligation to be polite, and then left the men alone.

"A woman named Claudia Davis was here on July seventh," Carella said. "Apparently she had her hair done by you. Can you tell us what you remember about her?"

"Miss Davis, Miss Davis," Mr. Sam said, touching his high forehead in an attempt at visual shorthand, trying to convey the concept of thought without having to do the accompanying brainwork. "Let me see, Miss Davis, Miss Davis."

"Yes."

"Yes, Miss Davis. A very pretty blonde."

"No," Carella said. He shook his head. "A brunette. You're thinking of the wrong person."

"No, I'm thinking of the right person," Mr. Sam said. He tapped his temple with one extended forefinger, another piece of visual abbreviation. "I remember. Claudia Davis. A blonde."

"A brunette," Carella insisted, and he kept watching Mr. Sam.

"When she left. But when she came, a blonde."

"What?" Hawes said.

"She was a blonde, a very pretty, natural blonde. It is rare. Natural blondness, I mean. I couldn't understand why she wanted to change the color."

"You dyed her hair?" Hawes asked.

"That is correct."

"Did she say *why* she wanted to be a brunette?"

"No, sir. I argued with her. I said, 'You have *beaut*-tiful hair, I can do *mar*-velous things with this hair of yours. You are a *blonde*, my dear, there are drab women who come in here every day of the week and *beg* to be turned into blondes.' No. She would not listen. I dyed it for her." Mr. Sam seemed to become offended by the idea all over again. He looked at the detectives as if they had been responsible for the stubbornness of Claudia Davis.

"What else did you do for her, Mr. Sam?" Carella asked.

"The dye, a cut, and a set. And I believe one of the girls gave her a facial and a manicure."

"What do you mean by a cut? Was her hair long when she came here?"

"Yes, beautiful long blond hair. She wanted it cut. I cut it." Mr. Sam shook his head. "A pity. She looked terrible. I don't usually say this about someone I work on, but she walked out of here looking terrible. You would hardly recognize her as the same pretty blonde who came in not three hours before."

"Maybe that was the idea," Carella said.

"I beg your pardon?"

"Forget it. Thank you, Mr. Sam. We know you're busy."

In the street outside Hawes said, "You knew before we went in there, didn't you, Mr. Steve?"

"I suspected, Mr. Cotton, I suspected. Come on, let's get back to the squad."

XIV

They kicked it around like a bunch of advertising executives. They sat in Lieutenant Byrnes' office and tried to find out how the cookie crumbled and which way the Tootsie rolled. They were just throwing out a life preserver to see if anyone grabbed at it, that's all. What they were doing, you see, was running up the flag to see if anyone saluted, that's all. The lieutenant's office was a four-window office because he was top man in this particular combine. It was a very elegant office. It had an electric fan all its own, and a big wide desk. It got cross ventilation from the street. It was really very pleasant. Well, to tell the truth, it was a pretty ratty office in which to be holding a top-level meeting, but it was the best the precinct had to offer. And after a while you got used to the chipping paint and the soiled walls and the bad lighting and the stench of urine from the men's room down the hall. Peter Byrnes didn't work for B.B.D.&O. He worked for the city. Somehow, there was a difference.

"I just put in a call to Irene Miller," Carella said. "I asked her to describe Claudia Davis to me, and she went through it all over again. Short dark hair, shy, plain. Then I asked her to describe the cousin, Josie Thompson." Carella nodded glumly. "Guess what?"

"A pretty girl," Hawes said. "A pretty girl with long blond hair."

"Sure. Why, Mrs. Miller practically spelled it out the first time we talked to her. It's all there in the report. She said they were like black and white in looks and personality. Black and white, sure. A brunette and a goddamn blond!"

"That explains the yellow," Hawes said.

"What yellow?"

"Courtenoy. He said he saw a patch of yellow breaking the surface. He wasn't talking about her clothes, Steve. He was talking about her *hair*."

"It explains a lot of things," Carella said. "It explains why shy Claudia Davis was preparing for her European trip by purchasing baby doll nightgowns and Bikini bathing suits. And it explains why the undertaker up there referred to Claudia as a pretty girl. And it explains why our necropsy report said she was thirty when everybody talked about her as if she were much younger."

"The girl who drowned wasn't Josie, huh?" Meyer said. "You figure she was Claudia."

"Damn right I figure she was Claudia."

"And you figure she cut her hair afterward, and dyed it, and took her cousin's name, and tried to pass as her cousin until she could get out of the country, huh?" Meyer said.

"Why?" Byrnes said. He was a compact man with a compact bullet head and a chunky economical body. He did not like to waste time or words.

"Because the trust income was in Claudia's name. Because Josie didn't have a dime of her own."

"She could have collected on her cousin's insurance policy," Meyer said.

"Sure, but that would have been the end of it. The trust called for those stocks to be turned over to U.C.L.A. if Claudia died. A college, for God's sake! How do you suppose Josie felt about that? Look, I'm not trying to hang a homicide on her. I just think she took advantage of a damn good situation. Claudia was in that boat alone. When she fell over the side, Josie really tried to rescue her, no question about it. But she missed, and Claudia drowned. Okay. Josie went all to pieces, couldn't talk straight, crying, sobbing, real hysterical woman, we've seen them before. But came the dawn. And with the dawn, Josie began thinking. They were away from the city, strangers in a strange town. Claudia had drowned but no one *knew* that she was Claudia. No one but Josie. She had no identification on her, remember? Her purse was in the car. Okay. If Josie identified her cousin correctly, she'd collect twenty-five grand on the insurance policy, and then all that stock would be turned over to the college, and that would be the end of the gravy train. But suppose, just suppose Josie told the police the girl in the lake was Josie Thompson? Suppose she said, 'I, Claudia Davis, tell you that girl who drowned is my cousin, Josie Thompson'?"

Hawes nodded. "Then she'd still collect on an insurance policy, and also fall heir to those fat security dividends coming in."

"Right. What does it take to cash a dividend check? A bank account, that's all. A bank account with an established signature. So all she had to do was open one, sign her name as Claudia Davis, and then endorse every dividend check that came in exactly the same way."

"Which explains the new account," Meyer said. "She couldn't use Claudia's old account because the bank undoubtedly knew both Claudia *and* her signature. So Josie had to forfeit the sixty grand at Highland Trust and start from scratch."

"And while she was building a new identity and a new fortune," Hawes said, "just to make sure Claudia's few friends forgot all about her, Josie was running off to Europe. She may have planned to stay there for years."

"It all ties in," Carella said. "Claudia had a driver's license. She was the one who drove the car away from Stewart City. But Josie had to hire a chauffeur to take her back."

"And would Claudia, who was so meticulous about money matters, have kept so many people waiting for payment?" Hawes said. "No, sir. That was Josie. And Josie was broke, Josie was waiting for that insurance policy to pay off so she could settle those debts and get the hell out of the country."

"Well, I admit it adds up," Meyer said.

Peter Byrnes never wasted words. "Who cashed that twenty-five thousand-dollar check for Josie?" he said.

There was silence in the room.

"Who's got that missing five grand?" he said.

There was another silence.

"Who *killed* Josie?" he said.

XV

Jeremiah Dodd of the Security Insurance Corporation, Inc., did not call until two days later. He asked to speak to Detective Carella, and when he got him on the phone, he said, "Mr. Carella, I've just heard from San Francisco on that check."

"What check?" Carella asked. He had been interrogating a witness to a knifing in a grocery store on Culver Avenue. The Claudia Davis or rather the Josie Thompson Case was not quite yet in the Open File, but it was ready to be dumped there, and was truly the farthest thing from Carella's mind at the moment.

"The check was paid to Claudia Davis," Dodd said.

"Oh, yes. Who cashed it?"

"Well, there are two endorsements on the back. One was made by Claudia Davis, of course. The other was made by an outfit called Leslie Summers, Inc. It's a regular company stamp marked 'For Deposit Only' and signed by one of the officers."

"Have any idea what sort of a company that is?" Carella asked.

"Yes," Dodd said. "They handle foreign exchange."

"Thank you," Carella said.

He went there with Bert Kling later that afternoon. He went with Kling completely by chance and only because Kling was heading downtown to buy his mother a birthday gift and offered Carella a ride. When they parked the car, Kling asked, "How long will this take, Steve?"

"Few minutes, I guess."

"Want to meet me back here?"

"Well, I'll be at 720 Hall, Leslie Summers, Inc. If you're through before me, come on over."

"Okay, I'll see you," Kling said.

They parted on Hall Avenue without shaking hands. Carella found the street-level office of Leslie Summers, Inc., and walked in. A counter ran the length of the room, and there were several girls behind it. One of the girls was speaking to a customer in French and another was talking Italian to a man who wanted lire in exchange for dollars. A board behind the desk quoted the current exchange rate for countries all over the world. Carella got in line and waited. When he reached the counter, the girl who'd been speaking French said, "Yes, sir?"

"I'm a detective," Carella said. He opened his wallet to where his shield was pinned to the leather. "You cashed a check for Miss Claudia Davis sometime in July. An insurance-company check for twenty-five thousand dollars. Would you happen to remember it?"

"No, sir, I don't think I handled it."

"Would you check around and see who did, please?"

The girl held a brief consultation with the other girls, and then walked to a desk behind which sat a corpulent, balding man with a razor-thin mustache. They talked with each other for a full five minutes. The man kept waving his hands. The girl kept trying to explain about the insurance-company check. The bell over the front door sounded. Bert Kling came in, looked around, saw Carella, and joined him at the counter.

"All done?" Carella asked.

"Yeah, I bought her a charm for her bracelet. How about you?"

"They're holding a summit meeting," Carella said.

The fat man waddled over to the counter. "What is the trouble?" he asked Carella.

"No trouble. Did you cash a check for twenty-five thousand dollars?"

"Yes. Is the check no good?"

"It's a good check."

"It looked like a good check. It was an insurance-company check. The young lady waited while we called the company. They said it was bona fide and we should accept it. Was it a bad check?"

"No, no, it was fine."

"She had identification. It all seemed very proper."

"What did she show you?"

"A driver's license or a passport is what we usually require. But she had neither. We accepted her birth certificate. After all, we *did* call the company. Is the check no good?"

"It's fine. But the check was for twenty-five thousand, and we're trying to find out what happened to five thousand of . . ."

"Oh, yes. The francs."

"What?"

"She bought five thousand dollars' worth of French francs," the fat man said. "She was going abroad?"

"Yes, she was going abroad," Carella said. He sighed heavily. "Well, that's that, I guess."

"It all seemed very proper," the fat man insisted.

"Oh, it was, it was. Thank you. Come on, Bert."

They walked down Hall Avenue in silence.

"Beats me," Carella said.

"What's that, Steve?"

"This case." He sighed again. "Oh, what the hell!"

"Yeah, let's get some coffee. What was all that business about the francs?"

"She bought five thousand dollars' worth of francs," Carella said.

"The French are getting a big play lately, huh?" Kling said, smiling. "Here's a place. This look okay?"

"Yeah, fine." Carella pulled open the door of the luncheonette. "What do you mean, Bert?"

"With the francs."

"What about them?"

"The exchange rate must be very good."

"I don't get you."

"You know. All those francs kicking around."

"Bert, what the hell are you talking about?"

"Weren't you with me? Last Wednesday?"

"With you where?"

"The line-up. I thought you were with me."

"No, I wasn't," Carella said tiredly.

"Oh, well, that's why."

"That's why what? Bert, for the love of . . ."

"That's why you don't remember him."

"Who?"

"The punk they brought in on that burglary pickup. They found five grand in French francs in his apartment."

Carella felt as if he'd just been hit by a truck.

XVI

It had been crazy from the beginning. Some of them are like that. The girl had looked black, but she was really white. They thought she was Claudia Davis, but she was Josie Thompson. And they had been looking for a murderer when all there happened to be was a burglar.

They brought him up from his cell where he was awaiting trial for Burglary One. He came up in an elevator with a police escort. The police van had dropped him off at the side door of the Criminal Courts Building, and he had entered the corridor under guard and been marched down through the connecting tunnel and into the building that housed the district attorney's office, and then taken into the elevator. The door of the elevator opened into a tiny room upstairs. The other door of the room was locked from the outside and a sign on it read No Admittance. The patrolman who'd brought Ralph Reynolds up to the interrogation room stood with his back against the elevator door all the while the detectives talked to him, and his right hand was on the butt of his Police Special.

"I never heard of her," Reynolds said.

"Claudia Davis," Carella said. "Or Josie Thompson. Take your choice."

"I don't know either one of them. What the hell *is* this? You got me on a burglary rap, now you try to pull in everything was ever done in this city?"

"Who said anything was done, Reynolds?"

"If nothing was done, why'd you drag me up here?"

"They found five thousand bucks in French francs in your pad, Reynolds. Where'd you get it?"

"Who wants to know?"

"Don't get snotty, Reynolds! Where'd you get that money?"

"A guy owed it to me. He paid me in francs. He was a French guy."

"What's his name?"

"I can't remember."

"You'd better start trying."

"Pierre something."

"Pierre what?" Meyer said.

"Pierre La Salle, something like that. I didn't know him too good."

"But you lent him five grand, huh?"

"Yeah."

"What were you doing on the night of August first?"

"Why? What happened on August first?"

"You tell us."

"I don't know what I was doing."

"Were you working?"

"I'm unemployed."

"You know what we mean!"

"No. What do you mean?"

"Were you breaking into apartments?"

"No."

"Speak up! Yes or no?"

"I said no."

"He's lying, Steve," Meyer said.

"Sure he is."

"Yeah, sure I am. Look, cop, you got nothing on me but Burglary One, if that. And that you gotta prove in court. So stop trying to hang anthing else on me. You ain't got a chance."

"Not unless those prints check out," Carella said quickly.

"What prints?"

"The prints we found on the dead girl's throat," Carella lied.

"I was wearing . . . !"

The small room went as still as death.

Reynolds sighed heavily. He looked at the floor.

"You want to tell us?"

"No," he said. "Go to hell."

He finally told them. After twelve hours of repeated questioning he finally broke down. He hadn't meant to kill her, he said. He didn't even know anybody was in the apartment. He had looked in the bedroom, and the bed was empty. He hadn't seen her asleep in one of the chairs, fully dressed. He had found the French money in a big jar on one of the shelves over the sink. He had taken the money and then accidentally dropped the jar, and she woke up and came into the room and saw him and began screaming. So he grabbed her by the throat. He only meant to shut her up. But she kept struggling. She was very strong. He kept holding on, but only to shut her up. She kept struggling, so he had to hold on. She kept struggling as if . . . as if he'd really been trying to kill her, as if she didn't want to lose her life. But that was manslaughter, wasn't it? He wasn't trying to kill her. That wasn't homicide, was it?

"I didn't mean to kill her!" he shouted as they took him into the elevator. "She began screaming! I'm not a killer. Look at me! Do I look like a killer?" And then, as the elevator began dropping to the basement, he shouted, "I'm a burglar!" as if proud of his profession, as if stating that he was something more than a common thief, a trained workman, a skilled artisan. "I'm not a killer! I'm a burglar!" he screamed. "I'm not a killer! I'm not a killer!" And his voice echoed down the elevator shaft as the car dropped to the basement and the waiting van.

They sat in the small room for several moments after he was gone.

"Hot in here," Meyer said.

"Yeah." Carella nodded.

"What's the matter?"

"Nothing."

"Maybe he's right," Meyer said. "Maybe he's only a burglar."

"He stopped being that the minute he stole a life, Meyer."

"Josie Thompson stole a life, too."

"No," Carella said. He shook his head. "She only borrowed one. There's a difference, Meyer."

The room went silent.

"You feel like some coffee?" Meyer asked.

"Sure."

They took the elevator down and then walked out into the brilliant August sunshine. The streets were teeming with life. They walked into the human swarm, but they were curiously silent.

At last Carella said, "I guess I think she shouldn't be dead. I guess I think that someone who tried so hard to make a life shouldn't have had it taken away from her."

"Meyer put his hand on Carella's shoulder. "Listen," he said earnestly. "It's a job. It's only a job."

"Sure," Carella said. "It's only a job."

THE SOUND OF MURDER
by Donald E. Westlake

Detective Abraham Levine of Brooklyn's Forty-Third Precinct sat at his desk in the squadroom and longed for a cigarette. The fingers of his left hand kept closing and clenching, feeling awkward without the paper-rolled tube of tobacco. He held a pencil for a while but unconsciously brought it to his mouth. He didn't realize what he was doing till he tasted the gritty staleness of the eraser. Then he put the pencil away in a drawer, and tried unsuccessfully to concentrate on the national news in the news magazine.

The world conspired against a man who tried to give up smoking. All around him were other people puffing cigarettes casually and unconcernedly, not making any fuss about it at all, making by their very nonchalance his own grim reasons for giving them up seem silly and hypersensitive. If he isolated himself from other smokers with the aid of television or radio, the cigarette commercials with their erotic smoking and their catchy jingles would surely drive him mad. Also, he would find that the most frequent sentence in popular fiction was, "He lit another cigarette." Statesmen and entertainers seemed inevitably to be smoking whenever news photographers snapped them for posterity, and even the news items were against him: He had just reread for the third time an announcement to the world that Pope John XXIII was the first Prelate of the Roman Catholic Church to smoke cigarettes in public.

Levine closed the magazine in irritation, and from the cover smiled at him the Governor of a midwestern state, cigarette in F.D.R. cigarette-holder at a jaunty angle in his mouth. Levine closed his eyes, saddened by the knowledge that he had turned himself at this late date into a comic character. A grown man who tries to give up smoking *is* comic, a Robert Benchley or a W.C. Fields, bumbling along, plagued by trivia, his life an endless gauntlet of minor crises. *They could do a one-reeler on me*, Levine thought. *A great little comedy. Laurel without Hardy. Because Hardy died of a heart attack.*

Abraham Levine, at fifty-three years of age, was twenty-four years a cop and eight years into the heart-attack range. When he went to bed at night, he kept himself awake by listening to the silence that replaced every eighth or ninth beat of his heart. When he had to climb stairs or lift anything heavy, he was acutely conscious of the labored heaviness of his breathing and of the way those missed heartbeats came closer and closer together, every seventh beat and then every sixth and then every fifth—

Some day, he knew, his heart would skip two beats in a row, and on that day Abraham Levine would stop, because there wouldn't be any third beat. None at all, not ever.

Four months ago, he'd gone to the doctor, and the doctor had checked him over very carefully, and he had submitted to it feeling like an aging auto brought to a mechanic by an owner who wanted to know whether it was worth while to fix the old boat up or should he just junk the thing and get another. (In the house next door to his, a baby cried every night lately. The new model, crying for the old and the obsolete to get off the road.)

So he'd gone to the doctor, and the doctor had told him not to worry. He had that little skip in his heartbeat, but that wasn't anything dangerous, lots of people had that. And his blood pressure was a little high, but not much, not enough to concern himself about. So the doctor told him he was healthy, and collected his fee, and Levine left, unconvinced.

So when he went back again three days ago, still frightened by the skip and the shortness of breath and the occasional chest cramps when he was excited or afraid, the doctor had told him the same things all over again, and had added, "If you really want to do something for that heart of yours, you can give up smoking."

He hadn't had a cigarette since, and for the first time in his life he was beginning really to understand the wails of the arrested junkies, locked away in a cell with nothing to ease their craving. He was beginning to be ashamed of himself, for having become so completely dependent on something so useless and so harmful. Three days now. Comic or not, he was going to make it.

Opening his eyes, he glared at the cigarette-smoking Governor and shoved the magazine into a drawer. Then he looked around the squadroom, empty except for himself and his partner, Crawley, sitting over there smoking contentedly at his desk by the filing cabinet as he worked on a report. Rizzo and McFarlane, and the other two detectives on this shift, were out on a call but would probably be back soon. Levine longed for the phone to ring, for something to happen to distract him, to keep mind and hands occupied and forgetful of cigarettes. He looked around the room, at a loss, and his left hand clenched and closed on the desk, lonely and incomplete.

When the rapping came at the door, it was so faint that Levine barely heard it, and Crawley didn't even look up. But any sound at all would have attracted Levine's straining attention. He looked over, saw a foreshortened shadow against the frosted glass of the door, and called, "Come in."

Crawley looked up. "What?"

"Someone at the door." Levine called out again, and this time the doorknob hesitantly turned, and a child walked in.

It was a little girl of about ten, in a frilly frock of pale pink, with a flared skirt, with gold-buckled black shoes and ribbed white socks. Her hair was pale blonde, combed and brushed and shampooed to gleaming cleanliness, brushed back from her forehead and held by a pink bow atop her head, then cascading straight down her back nearly to her waist. Her eyes were huge and bright blue, her face a creamy oval. She was a little girl in an ad for children's clothing in the *Sunday Times*. She was a story illustration in *Ladies' Home Journal*. She was Alice in Blunderland, gazing with wide-eyed curious innocence into the bullpen, the squadroom, the home and office of the detectives of the Forty-Third Precinct, the men whose job it was to catch the stupid and the nasty so that other men could punish them.

She saw, looking into this brutal room, two men and a lot of old furniture.

It was inevitably to Levine that the little girl spoke: "May I come in?" Her voice was as faint as her tapping on the door had been. She was poised to flee at the first loud noise.

Levine automatically lowered his own voice when he answered. "Of course. Come on in. Sit over here." He motioned at the straight-backed wooden chair beside his desk.

The girl crossed the threshold, carefully closed the door again behind her, and came on silent feet across the room, glancing sidelong at Crawley, then establishing herself on the edge of the chair, her toes touching the floor, still ready for flight at any second. She studied Levine. "I want to talk to a detective," she said. "Are you a detective?"

Levine nodded. "Yes, I am."

"My name," she told him solemnly, "is Amy Thornbridge Walker. I live at 717 Prospect Park West, apartment 4-A. I want to report a murder, a quite recent murder."

"A murder?"

"My mother," she said, just as solemnly, "murdered my stepfather."

Levine glanced over at Crawley, who screwed his face up in an expression meant to say, "She's a nut. Hear her out, and then she'll go home. What else can you do?"

There was nothing else he could do. He looked at Amy Thornbridge Walker again. "Tell me about it," he said. "When did it happen?"

"Two weeks ago Thursday," she said. "November 27th. At two-thirty P.M."

Her earnest calm called for belief. But children with wild stories were not unknown to the precinct. Children came in with reports of dead bodies in alleys, flying saucers on rooftops, counterfeiters in basement apartments, kidnappers in black trucks—And once out of a thousand times what the child reported was real and not the product of a young imagination on a spree. More to save the little girl's feelings than for any other reason, therefore, Levine drew to him a pencil and a sheet of paper and took down what she told him. He said, "What's your mother's name?"

"Gloria Thornbridge Walker," she said. "And my stepfather was Albert Walker. He was an attorney."

To the side, Crawley was smiling faintly at the girl's conscious formality. Levine solemnly wrote down the names, and said, "Was your father's name Thornbridge, is that it?"

"Yes. Jason Thornbridge. He died when I was very small. I think my mother killed him, too, but I'm not absolutely sure."

"I see. But you *are* absolutely sure that your mother killed Albert Walker."

"My stepfather. Yes. My first father was supposed to have drowned by accident in Lake Champlain, which I consider very unlikely, as he was an excellent swimmer."

Levine reached into his shirt pocket, found no cigarettes there, and suddenly realized what he was doing. Irritation washed over him, but he carefully kept it from showing in his face or voice as he said, "How long have you thought that your mother killed your rea—your first father?"

"I'd never thought about it at all," she said, "until she murdered my stepfather. Naturally, I then started thinking about it."

Crawley coughed, and lit a fresh cigarette, keeping his hands up in front of his mouth. Levine said, "Did he die of drowning, too?"

"No. My stepfather wasn't athletic at all. In fact, he was nearly an invalid for the last six months of his life."

"Then how did your mother kill him?"

"She made a loud noise at him," she said calmly.

Levine's pencil stopped its motion. He looked at her searchingly, but found no trace of humor in her eyes or mouth. If she had come up here as a joke—on a bet, say from her schoolmates—then she was a fine little actress, for no sign of the joke was on her face at all.

Though how could he really tell? Levine, a childless man with a barren wife, had found it difficult over the years to communicate with the very young. A part of it, of course, was an envy he couldn't help, in the knowledge that these children could run and play with no frightening shortness of breath or tightness of chest, that they could sleep at night in their beds with no thought for the dull thudding of their hearts, that they would be alive and knowing for years and decades, for *decades*, after he himself had ceased to exist.

Before he could formulate an answer to what she'd said, the little girl jounced off the chair with the graceful gracelessness of the young and said, "I can't stay any longer. I stopped here on my way home from school. If my mother found out that I knew, and that I had told the police, she might try to murder me, too." She turned all at once and studied Crawley severely. "I am not a silly little girl," she told him. "And I am not telling a lie or making a joke. My mother murdered my stepfather, and I came in here and reported it. That's what I'm supposed to do. You aren't supposed to believe me right away, but you are supposed to investigate and find out whether or not I've told you the truth. And I have told you the truth." She turned suddenly back to Levine, an angry little girl—no, not angry, *definite*—a definite little girl filled with stern formality and a child's sense of rightness and duty. "My stepfather," she said, "was a very good man. My mother is a bad woman. You find out what she did, and punish her." She nodded briefly, as though to punctuate what she'd said, and marched to the door, reaching it as Rizzo and McFarlane came in. They looked down at her in surprise, and she stepped past them and out to the hall, closing the door fater her.

Rizzo looked at Levine and jerked his thumb at the door. "What was that?"

It was Crawley who answered. "She came in to report a murder," he said. "Her Mommy killed her Daddy by making a great big noise at him."

Rizzo frowned. "Come again?"

"I'll check it out," said Levine. Not believing the girl's story, he still felt the impact of her demand on him that he do his duty. All it would take was a few phone calls. While Crawley recounted the episode at great length to Rizzo, and McFarlane took up his favorite squadroom position, seated at his desk with the chair canted back and his feet atop the desk, Levine picked up his phone and dialed the *New York Times*. He identified himself and said what he wanted, was connected to the right department, and after a few minutes the November 28th obituary notice on Albert Walker was read to him. Cause of death: a heart attack. Mortician: Junius Merriman. An even briefer call to Merriman gave him the name of Albert Walker's doctor, Henry Sheffield. Levine thanked Merriman, assured him there was no problem, and got out the Brooklyn yellow pages to find Sheffield's number. He dialed, spoke to a nurse, and finally got Sheffield.

"I can't understand," Sheffield told him, "why the police would be interested in the case. It was heart failure, pure and simple. What seems to be the problem?"

"There's no problem," Levine told him. "Just checking it out. Was this a sudden attack? Had he had any heart trouble before?"

"Yes, he'd suffered a coronary attack about seven months ago. The second attack was more severe, and he hadn't really recovered as yet from the first. There certainly wasn't anything else to it, if that's what you're getting at."

"I didn't mean to imply anything like that," said Levine. "By the way, were you Mrs. Walker's first husband's doctor, too?"

"No, I wasn't. His name was Thornbridge, wasn't it? I never met the man. Is there some sort of question about him?"

"No, not at all." Levine evaded a few more questions, then hung up, his duty done. He turned to Crawley and shook his head. "Nothing to—"

A sudden crash behind him froze the words in his throat. He half-rose from the chair, mouth wide open, face paling as the blood rushed from his head, his nerves and muscles stiff and tingling.

It was over in a second, and he sank back into the chair, turning around to see what had happened. McFarlane was sheepishly picking himself up from the floor, his chair lying on its back beside him. He grinned shakily at Levine." Leaned back too far that time," he said.

"Don't do that," said Levine, his voice shaky. He touched the back of his hand to his forehead, feeling cold perspiration slick against the skin. He was trembling all over. Once again, he reached to his shirt pocket for a cigarette, and this time felt an instant of panic when he found the pocket empty. He pressed the palm of his hand to the pocket, and beneath pocket and skin he felt the thrumming of his heart, and automatically counted the beats. Thum, thum, *skip*, thum, thum, thum, thum, thum, *skip*, thum, thum,—

On the sixth beat, the *sixth* beat. He sat there listening, hand pressed to his chest, and gradually the agitation subsided and the skip came every seventh beat and then every eighth beat, and then he could dare to move again.

He licked his lips, needing a cigarette now more than at any other time in the last three days, more than he could ever remember needing a cigarette at any time in his whole life.

His resolve crumbled. Shamefacedly, he turned to his partner, "Jack, do you have a cigarette?"

Crawley looked away from McFarlane, who was checking himself for damage. "I thought you were giving them up, Abe," he said.

"Not around here. Please, Jack."

"Sure." Crawley tossed him his pack.

Levine caught the pack, shook out one cigarette,

threw the rest back to Crawley. He took a book of matches from the desk drawer, put the cigarette in his mouth, feeling the comforting familiarity of it between his lips, and struck a match. He held the match up, then sat looking at the flame, struck by a sudden thought.

Albert Walker had died of a heart attack. "She made a loud noise at him." "The second attack was more severe, and he hadn't really recovered as yet from the first."

He shook the match out, took the cigarette from between his lips. It had been every sixth beat there for a while, after the loud noise of McFarlane's backward dive.

Had Gloria Thornbridge Walker *really* killed Albert Walker?

Would Abraham Levine *really* kill Abraham Levine?

The second question was easier to answer. Levine opened the desk drawer and dropped the cigarette and matches into it.

The first question he didn't try to answer at all. He would sleep on it. Right now, he wasn't thinking straight enough.

At dinner that night, he talked it over with his wife. "Peg," he said, "I've got a problem."

"A problem?" She looked up in surprise, a short solid stout woman three years her husband's junior, her iron-gray hair rigidly curled in a home permanent. "If you're coming to me," she said, "it must be awful."

He smiled, nodding. "It is." It was rare for him to talk about his job with his wife. The younger men, he knew, discussed their work with their wives as a matter of course, expecting and receiving suggestions and ideas and advice. But he was a product of an older upbringing, and still believed instinctively that women should be shielded from the more brutal aspects of life. It was only when the problem was one he couldn't discuss with

Crawley that he turned to Peg for someone to talk to. "I'm getting old," he said suddenly, thinking of the differences between himself and the younger men.

She laughed. "That's your problem? Don't feel lonely, Abe, it happens to all kinds of people. Have some more gravy."

"Let me tell you," he said. "A little girl came in today, maybe ten years old, dressed nicely, polite, very intelligent. She wanted to report that her mother had killed her stepfather."

"A little girl?" She sounded shocked. She too believed that there were those who should be shielded from the more brutal aspects of life, but with her the shielded ones were children. "A little girl? A thing like that?"

"Wait," he said. "Let me tell you. I called the doctor and he said it was a heart attack. The stepfather—Mr. Walker—he'd had one attack already, and the second one on top of it killed him."

"But the little girl blames the mother?" Peg leaned forward. "Psychological, you think?"

"I don't know. I asked her how her mother had done the killing, and she said her mother made a loud noise at her father."

"A joke." She shook her head. "These children today, I don't know where they get their ideas. All this on the TV—"

"Maybe," he said. "I don't know. A man with a bad heart, bedridden, an invalid. A sudden shock, a loud noise, it might do it, bring on that second attack."

"What else did this little girl say?"

"That's all. Her stepfather was good, and her mother was bad, and she'd stopped off on her way home from school. She only had a minute, because she didn't want her mother to know what she was doing."

"You let her go? You didn't question her?"

Levine shrugged. "I didn't believe her," he said. "You know the imagination children have."

"But now?"

"Now, I don't know." He held up his hand, two fingers extended. "Now," he said, "there's two questions in my mind. First, is the little girl right or wrong? Did her mother actually make a loud noise that killed her stepfather or not? And if she did, then question number two: Did she do it on purpose, or was it an accident?" He waggled the two fingers and looked at his wife. "Do you see? Maybe the little girl is right, and her mother actually did cause the death, but not intentionally. If so, I don't want to make things worse for the mother by dragging it into the open. Maybe the little girl is wrong altogether, and if so it would be best to just let the whole thing slide. But maybe she's right, and it *was* murder, and then that child is in danger, because if I don't do anything, she'll try some other way, and the mother will find out."

Peg shook her head. "I don't like that, a little girl like that. Could she defend herself? A woman to kill her husband, a woman like that could kill her child just as easy. I don't like that at all, Abe."

"Neither do I." He reached for the coffee cup, drank. "The question is, what do I do?"

She shook her head again. "A child like that," she said. "A woman like that. And then again, maybe not." She looked at her husband. "For right now," she said, "you eat. We can think about it."

For the rest of dinner they discussed other things. After the meal, as usual, the craving for a cigarette suddenly intensified, and he was unable to concentrate on anything but his resolution. They watched television during the evening, and by bedtime he still hadn't made a decision. Getting ready for bed, Peg suddenly said, "The little girl. You've been thinking?"

"I'll sleep on it," he said. "Maybe in the morning. Peg, I am longing for a cigarette."

"Nails in your coffin," she said bluntly. He blinked, and went away silently to brush his teeth.

The lights turned out, they lay together in the double bed which now, with age, had a pronounced sag toward the middle, rolling them together. But it was a cold night out, a good night to lie close together and feel the warmth of life. Levine closed his eyes and drifted slowly toward sleep.

A sudden sound shook him awake. He blinked rapidly, staring up in the darkness at the ceiling, startled, disoriented, not knowing what it was. But then the sound came again, and he exhaled, releasing held breath. It was the baby from next door, crying.

Move over, world, and give us room, he thought, giving words to the baby's cries. *Make way for the new.*

And they're right, he thought. *We've got to take care of them, and guide them, and then make way for them. They're absolutely right.*

I've got to do something for that little girl, he thought.

In the morning, Levine talked to Crawley. He sat in the client's chair, beside Crawley's desk. "About that little girl," he said.

"You, too? I got to thinking about it myself, last night."

"We ought to check it out," Levine told him.

"I know. I figure I ought to look up the death of the first father. Jason Thornbridge, wasn't it?"

"Good," said Levine. "I was thinking of going to her school, talking to the teacher. If she's the kind of child who makes up wild stories all the time, then that's that, you know what I mean?"

"Sure. You know what school she's in?"

"Lathmore Elementary, over on Third."

Crawley frowned, trying to remember. "She tell you that? I didn't hear it if she did."

"No, she didn't. But it's the only one it could be." Levine grinned sheepishly. "I'm pulling a Sherlock Holmes," he said. "She told us she'd stopped in on her way home from school. So she was walking home, and there's only three schools in the right direction—so we'd be between them and Prospect Park—but they're close enough for her to walk." He checked them off on his fingers. "There's St. Aloysius, but she wasn't in a school uniform. There's PS 118, but with a Prospect Park West address and the clothing she was wearing and her good manners, she doesn't attend public school. So that leaves Lathmore."

"Okay, Sherlock," said Crawley. "You go talk to the nice people at Lathmore. I'll dig into the Thornbridge thing."

"One of us," Levine told him, "ought to check this out with the Lieutenant first. Tell him what we want to do."

"Fine. Go ahead."

Levine scraped the fingers of his left hand together, embarrassment reminding him of his need for a cigarette. But this was day number four, and he was going to make it. "Jack," he said, "I think maybe you ought to be the one to talk to him."

"Why me? Why not you?"

"I think he has more respect for you."

Crawley snorted. "What the hell are you talking about?"

"No, I mean it, Jack." Levine grinned self-consciously. "If I told him about it, he might think I was just dramatizing it, getting emotional or something, and he'd say thumbs down. But you're the level headed type. If you tell him it's serious, he'll believe you."

"You're nuts," said Crawley.

"You *are* the level-headed type," Levine told him. "And I *am* too emotional."

"Flattery will get you everywhere. All right, go to school."

"Thanks, Jack."

Levine shrugged into his coat and plodded out of the squadroom, downstairs, and out to the sidewalk. Lathmore Elementary was three blocks away to the right, and he walked it. There was a smell of snow in the air, but the sky was still clear. Levine strolled along sniffing the snow-tang, his hands pushed deep into the pockets of his black overcoat. The desire for a smoke was less when he was outdoors, so he didn't hurry.

Lathmore Elementary, one of the myriad private schools which have sprung up to take the place of the enfeebled public school system long since emasculated by municipal politics, was housed in an old mansion on one of the neighborhood's better blocks. The building was mainly masonry, with curved buttresses and bay windows everywhere, looming three ivy-overgrown stories to a patchwork slate roof which dipped and angled and rose crazily around to no pattern at all. Gold letters on the wide glass pane over the double-doored entrance announced the building's new function, and just inside the doors an arrow on a wall was marked "OFFICE."

Levine didn't want to have to announce himself as a policeman, but the administrative receptionist was so officious and curious that he had no choice. It was the only way he could get to see Mrs. Pidgeon, the principal, without first explaining his mission in minute detail to the receptionist.

Mrs. Pidgeon was baffled, polite, terrified and defensive, but not very much of any of them. It was as though these four emotions were being held in readiness, for one of them to spring into action as soon as she found out exactly what it was a police officer could possibly want in Lathmore Elementary. Levine tried to explain as gently and vaguely as possible:

"I'd like to talk to one of your teachers," he said. "About a little girl, a student of yours."

"What about her?"

"She made a report to us yesterday," Levine told her. "It's difficult for us to check it out, and it might help if we knew a little more about her, what her attitudes are, things like that."

Defensiveness began to edge to the fore in Mrs. Pidgeon's attitude. "What sort of report?"

"I'm sorry," said Levine. "If there's nothing to it, it would be better not to spread it."

"Something about this school?"

"Oh, no," said Levine, managing not to smile. "Not at all."

"Very well." Defensiveness receded, and a sort of cold politeness became more prominent. "You want to talk to her teacher, then."

"Yes."

"Her name?"

"Amy Walker. Amy Thornbridge Walker."

"Oh, yes!" Mrs. Pidgeon's face suddenly lit with pleasure, not at Levine but at his reminding her of that particular child. Then the pleasure gave way just as suddenly to renewed bafflement. "It's about Amy? *She* came to you yesterday?"

"That's right."

"Well." She looked helplessly around the room, aching to find out more but unable to find a question that would get around Levine's reticence. Finally, she gave up, and asked him to wait while she went for Miss Haskell, the fifth grade teacher. Levine stood as she left the room, then sank back into the maroon leather chair, feeling bulky and awkward in this hushed heavy-draped office.

He waited five minutes before Mrs. Pidgeon returned, this time with Miss Haskell in tow. Miss Haskell, unexpectedly, was a comfortable fortyish woman in a sensible suit and flat shoes, not the thin tall bird he'd expected. He acknowledged Mrs. Pidgeon's introduction, hastily rising again, and Mrs. Pidgeon pointedly said, "Try not to be too long, Mr. Levine. You may use my office."

"Thank you."

She left, and Levine and Miss Haskell stood facing each other in the middle of the room. He motioned at a chair. "Would you sit down, please?"

"Thank you. Mrs. Pidgeon said you wanted to ask me about Amy Walker."

"Yes, I want to know what kind of child she is, anything you can tell me about her."

Miss Haskell smiled. "I can tell you she's a brilliant and well-brought-up child," she said. "That she's the one I picked to be student in charge while I came down to talk to you. That she's always at least a month ahead of the rest of the class in reading the assignments, and that she's the most practical child I've ever met."

Levine reached to his cigarette pocket, cut the motion short, awkwardly returned his hand to his side. "Her father died two weeks ago, didn't he?"

"That's right."

"How did they get along, do you know? Amy and her father."

"She worshipped him. He was her stepfather actually, having married her mother only about a year ago, I believe. Amy doesn't remember her real father. Mr. Walker was the only father she knew, and having been without one for so long—" Miss Haskell spread her hands. "He was important to her," she finished.

"She took his death hard?"

"She was out of school for a week, inconsolable. She spent the time at her grandmother's, I understand. The grandmother caters to her, of course. I believe her mother had a doctor in twice."

"Yes, her mother." Levine didn't know what to do with his hands. He clasped them in front of him. "How do Amy and her mother get along?"

"Normally, so far as I know. There's never been any sign of discord between them that I've seen." She smiled again. "But my contact with Amy is limited to school hours, of course."

"You think there is discord?"

"No, not at all. I didn't mean to imply that. Just that I couldn't give you an expert answer to the question."

Levine nodded. "You're right. Is Amy a very imaginative child?"

"She's very self-sufficient in play, if that's what you mean."

"I was thinking about story-telling."

"Oh, a liar." She shook her head. "No, Amy isn't the tall tale type. A very practical little girl, really. Very dependable judgment. As I say, she's the one I left in charge of the class."

"She wouldn't be likely to come to us with a wild story she'd made up all by herself."

"Not at all. If Amy told you about something, it's almost certainly the truth."

Levine sighed. "Thank you," he said. "Thank you very much."

Miss Haskell rose to her feet. "Could you tell me what this wild story was? I might be able to help."

"I'd rather not," he said. "Not until we're sure, one way or the other."

"If I can be of any assistance—"

"Thank you," he said again. "You've already helped."

Back at the station, Levine entered the squadroom and hung up his coat. Crawley looked over from his desk and said, "You have all the luck, Abe. You missed the whirlwind."

"Whirlwind?"

"Amy's mama was here. Dr. Sheffield called her about you checking up on her husband's death, and just before she came over here she got a call from somebody at Lathmore Elementary, saying there was a cop there asking questions about her daughter. She didn't like us casting aspersions on her family."

"Aspersions?"

"That's what she said." Crawley grinned. "You're little Sir Echo this morning, aren't you?"

"I need a cigarette. What did the Lieutenant say?"

"She didn't talk to him. She talked to me."

"No, when you told him about the little girl's report."

"Oh. He said to take two days on it, and then let him know how it looked."

"Fine. How about Thornbridge?"

"Accidental death. Inquest said so. No question in anybody's mind. He went swimming too soon after lunch, got a stomach cramp, and drowned. What's the word on the little girl?"

"Her teacher says she's reliable. Practical and realistic. If she tells us something, it's so."

Crawley grimaced. "That isn't what I wanted to hear, Abe."

"It didn't overjoy me, either." Levine sat down at

his desk. "What did the mother have to say?"

"I had to spill it, Abe. About what her daughter reported."

"That's all right," he said. "Now we've got no choice. We've got to follow through. What was her reaction?"

"She didn't believe it."

Levine shrugged. "She had to, after she thought about it."

"Sure," said Crawley. "Then she was baffled. She didn't know why Amy would say such a thing."

"Was she home when her husband died?"

"She says no," Crawley flipped open a memo pad. "Somebody had to be with him all the time, but he didn't want a professional nurse. So when Amy came home from school that afternoon, the mother went to the supermarket. Her husband was alive when she left, and dead when she got back. Or so she says."

"She says Amy was the one who found him dead?"

"No. Amy was watching television. When the mother came home, she found him, and called the doctor."

"What about noises?"

"She didn't hear any, and doesn't have any idea what Amy means."

Levine sighed. "All right," he said. "We've got one timetable discrepancy. Amy says her mother was home and made a loud noise. The mother says she was out to the supermarket." His fingers strayed to his cigarette pocket, then went on to scratch his shoulder instead. "What do you think of the mother, Jack?"

"She's tough. She was mad, and she's used to having things her own way. I can't see her playing nursemaid. But she sure seemed baffled about why the kid would make such an accusation."

"I'll have to talk to Amy again," said Levine. "Once we've got both stories, we can see which one breaks down."

Crawley said, "I wonder if she'll try to shut the kid's mouth?"

"Let's not think about that yet. We've still got all day." He reached for the phone book and looked up the number of Lathmore Elementary.

Levine talked to the girl in Mrs. Pidgeon's office at eleven o'clock. At his request, they were left alone.

Amy was dressed as neatly as she had been yesterday, and seemed just as composed. Levine explained to her what had been done so far on the investigation, and that her mother had been told why the investigation was taking place. "I'm sorry, Amy," he said, "but we didn't have any choice. Your mother had to know."

Amy considered, solemn and formal. "I think it will be all right," she said. "She wouldn't dare try to hurt me now, with you investigating. It would be too obvious. My mother is very subtle, Mr. Levine."

Levine smiled, in spite of himself. "You have quite a vocabulary," he told her.

"I'm a very heavy reader," she explained. "Though it's difficult for me to get interesting books from the library. I'm too young, so I have to take books from the children's section." She smiled thinly. "I'll tell you a secret," she said. "I steal the ones I want to read, and then bring them back when I'm finished with them."

In a hurry, he thought, smiling, and remembered the baby next door. "I want to talk to you," he said, "about the day when your father died. Your mother said she went out to the store, and when she came back he was dead. What do you say?"

"Nonsense," she said, promptly. "*I* was the one who went out to the store. The minute I came home from school, she sent me out to the supermarket. But I came back too soon for her."

"Why?"

"Just as I was coming down the hall from the elevator, I heard a great clang sound from our apartment. Then it came again as I was opening the door. I went through the living room and saw my mother coming out of my stepfather's room. She was smiling. But then she saw me and suddenly looked terribly upset and told me something awful had happened, and she ran to the telephone to call Dr. Sheffield. She acted terribly agitated, and carried on just as though she really meant it. She fooled Dr. Sheffield completely."

"Why did you wait so long before coming to us?"

"I didn't know what to do." The solemn formality cracked all at once, and she was only a child after all, uncertain in an adult world. "I didn't think anyone would believe me, and I was afraid if Mother suspected what I knew, she might try to do something to me. But Monday in Civics Miss Haskell was talking about the duties of the different parts of government, firemen and policemen and everybody, and she said the duty of the police was to investigate crimes and see the guilty were punished. So yesterday I came and told you, because it didn't matter if you didn't believe me, you'd have to do your duty and investigate anyway."

Levine sighed. "All right," he said. "We're doing it. But we need more than just your word, you understand that, don't you? We need proof of some kind."

She nodded, serious and formal again.

"What store did you go to that day?" he asked her.

"A supermarket. The big one on Seventh Avenue."

"Do you know any of the clerks there? Would they recognize you?"

"I don't think so. It's a great big supermarket. I don't think they know any of their customers at all."

"Did you see anyone at all on your trip to the store or back, who would remember that it was you who went to the store and not your mother, and that it was that particular day?"

She considered, touching one finger to her lips as she concentrated, and finally shook her head. "I don't think so. I don't know any of the people in the neighborhood. Most of the people I know are my parents' friends or kids from school, and they live all over, not just around here."

The New York complication. In a smaller town, people know their neighbors, have some idea of the comings and goings around them. But in New York, next-door neighbors remain strangers for years. At least that was true in the apartment house sections, though less true in the quieter outlying sections like the neighborhood in which Levine lived.

Levine got to his feet. "We'll see what we can do," he said. "This clang you told me about. Do you have any idea what your mother used to make the noise?"

"No, I don't. I'm sorry. It sounded like a gong or something. I don't know what it could possibly have been."

"A tablespoon against the bottom of a pot? Something like that?"

"Oh, no. Much louder than that."

"And she didn't have anything in her hands when she came out of the bedroom?"

"No, nothing."

"Well, we'll see what we can do," he repeated. "You can go back to class now."

"Thank you," she said. "Thank you for helping me."

He smiled. "It's my duty," he said. "As you pointed out."

"You'd do it anyway, Mr. Levine," she said. "You're a very good man. Like my stepfather."

Levine touched the palm of his hand to his chest, over his heart. "Yes," he said. "In more ways than one, maybe. Well, you go back to class. Or, wait. There's one thing I can do for you."

She waited as he took a pencil and a small piece of memo paper from Mrs. Pidgeon's desk, and wrote on it the precinct phone number and his home phone number, marking which each was. "If you think there's any danger of any kind," he told her, "any trouble at all, you call me. At the precinct until four o'clock, and then at home after that."

"Thank you," she said. She folded the paper and tucked it away in the pocket of her skirt.

At a quarter to four, Levine and Crawley met again in the squadroom. When he'd come back in the morning from his talk with the little girl, Levine had found Crawley just back from having talked with Dr. Sheffield. It was Sheffield's opinion, Crawley had told him, that Amy was making the whole thing up, that her stepfather's death had been a severe shock and this was some sort of delayed reaction to it. Certainly he couldn't see any possibility that Mrs. Walker had actually murdered her husband, nor could he begin to guess at any motive for such an act.

Levine and Crawley had eaten lunch together in Wilton's, across the street from the station, and then had separated, both to try to find someone who had either seen Amy or her mother on the shopping trip the afternoon Mr. Walker had died. This, aside from the accusation of murder itself, was the only contradiction between their stories. Find proof that one was lying, and they'd have the full answer. So Levine had started at the market and Crawley at the apartment building, and they'd spent the entire afternoon up and down the neighborhood, asking their questions and getting only blank stares for answers.

Crawley was there already when Levine came slowly into the squadroom, worn from an entire afternoon on his feet, climaxed by the climb to the precinct's second floor. He looked at Crawley and shook his head. Crawley said, "Nothing? Same here. Not a damn thing."

Levine laboriously removed his overcoat and set it on the coatrack. "No one remembers," he said. "No one saw, no one knows anyone. It's a city of strangers we live in, Jack."

"It's been two weeks," said Crawley. "Their building has a doorman, but he can't remember that far back. He sees the same tenants go in and out every day, and he wouldn't be able to tell you for sure who went in or out yesterday, much less two weeks ago, he says."

Levine looked at the wall-clock. "She's home from school by now," he said.

"I wonder what they're saying to each other. If we could listen in, we'd know a hell of a lot more than we do now."

Levine shook his head. "No. Whether she's guilty or innocent, they're both saying the exact same things. The death is two weeks old. If Mrs. Walker did commit murder, she's used to the idea by now that she's gotten away with it. She'll deny everything Amy says, and try to convince the girl she's wrong. The same things in the same words as she'd use if she were innocent."

"What if she kills the kid?" Crawley asked him.

"She won't. If Amy were to disappear, or have an

accident, or be killed by an intruder, we'd know the truth at once. She can't take the chance. With her husband, all she had to do was fool a doctor who was inclined to believe her in the first place. Besides, the death was a strong possibility anyway. This time, she'd be killing a healthy ten-year-old, and she'd be trying to fool a couple of cops who wouldn't be inclined to believe her at all." Levine grinned. "The girl is probably safer now than she was before she ever came to us," he said. "Who knows what the mother might have been planning up till now?"

"All right, that's fine so far. But what do we do now?"

"Tomorrow, I want to take a look at the Walker apartment."

"Why not right now?"

"No. Let's give her a night to get rattled. Any evidence she hasn't removed in two weeks she isn't likely to think of now." Levine shrugged. "I don't expect to find anything," he said. "I want to look at the place because I can't think of anything else to do. All we have is the unsupported word of a ten-year old child. The body can't tell us anything, because there wasn't any murder weapon. Walker died of natural causes. Proving they were induced won't be the easiest job in the world."

"If only *somebody*," said Crawley angrily, "had seen that kid at the grocery store! That's the only chink in the wall, Abe, the only damn place we can get a grip."

"We can try again tomorrow," said Levine, "but I doubt we'll get anywhere." He looked up as the door opened, and Trent and Kasper came in, two of the men on the four to midnight shift. "Tomorrow," he repeated. "Maybe lightning will strike."

"Maybe," said Crawley.

Levine shrugged back into his overcoat and left the

office for the day. When he got home, he broke his normal habit and went straight into the house, not staying on the porch to read his paper. He went out to the kitchen and sat there, drinking coffee, while he filled Peg in on what little progress they'd made on the case during the day. She asked questions, and he answered them, offered suggestions and he mulled them over and rejected them, and throughout the evening, every once in a while, one or the other of them would find some other comment to make, but neither of them got anywhere. The girl seemed to be reasonably safe, at least for a while, but that was the best that could be said.

The baby next door was crying when they went to bed together at eleven o'clock. The baby kept him awake for a while, and his thoughts on the Walker death revolved and revolved, going nowhere. Once or twice during the evening, he had absent-mindedly reached for a cigarette, but had barely noticed the motion. His concentration and concern for Amy Walker and her mother was strong enough now to make him forget his earlier preoccupation with the problem of giving up smoking. Now, lying awake in the dark, the thought of cigarettes didn't even enter his head. He went over and over what the mother had said, what the daughter had told him, and gradually he drifted off into deep, sound sleep.

He awoke in a cold sweat, suddenly knowing the truth. It was as though he'd dreamed it, or someone had whispered it in his ear, and now he knew for sure.

She would kill tonight, and she would get away with it. He knew how she'd do it, and when, and there'd be no way to get her for it, no proof, nothing, no way at all.

He sat up, trembling, cold in the dark room, and

reached out to the nightstand for his cigarettes. He pawed around on the nightstand, and suddenly remembered, and pounded the nightstand with his fist in frustration and rage. She'd get away with it!

If he could get there in time—He could stop her, if he got there in time. He pushed the covers out of the way and climbed from the bed. Peg murmured in her sleep and burrowed deeper into the pillow. He gathered his clothes and crept from the bedroom.

He turned the light on in the living room. The clock over the television set read ten till one. There might still be time, she might be waiting until she was completely asleep. Unless she was going to do it with pills, something to help sleep, to make sleep a permanent, everlasting sure thing.

He grabbed the phone book and looked up the number of one of the private cab companies on Avenue L. He dialed, and told the dispatcher it was urgent, and the dispatcher said a car would be there in five minutes.

He dressed hurriedly, in the living room, then went out to the kitchen for pencil and paper, and left Peg a short note. "I had to go out for a while. Be back soon." In case she woke up. He left it on the nightstand.

A horn sounded briefly out front and he hurried to the front of the house, turning off lights. As he went trotting down the walk toward the cab, the baby next door cried out. He registered the sound, thought, *Baby next door*, and dismissed it from his mind. He had no time for extraneous thoughts, about babies or cigarettes or the rasp of his breathing from only this little exertion, running from the house. He gave the address, Prospect Park West, and sat back in the seat as the cab took off. It was a strange feeling, riding in a cab. He couldn't remember the last time he'd done it. It was a luxuriant feeling. To go so fast with such relaxing calm. If only it was fast enough.

It cost him four dollars, including the tip. If she was still alive, it was the bargain of the century. But as he hurried into the building and down the long narrow lobby to the elevators, the sound he'd heard as he'd left his home came back to him, he heard it again in his memory, and all at once he realized it hadn't been the baby next door at all. It had been the telephone.

He pressed the elevator button desperately, and the elevator slid slowly down to him from the eleventh floor. It had been the ring of the telephone.

So she'd made her move already. He was too late. When he'd left the house, he'd been too late.

The elevator doors opened, and he stepped in, pushed the button marked 4. He rode upward.

He could visualize that phone call. The little girl, hushed, terrified, whispering, beseeching. And Peg, half-awake, reading his note to her. And he was too late.

The door to apartment 4-A was ajar, the interior dark. He reached to his hip, but he'd been in too much of a hurry. The gun was at home, on the dresser.

He stepped across the threshold, cautiously, peering into the dark. Dim light spilled in from the hallway, showing him only this section of carpet near the door. The rest of the apartment was pitch black.

He felt the wall beside the door, found the light switch and clicked it on.

The light in the hall went out.

He tensed, the darkness now complete. A penny in the socket? And this was an old building, in which the tenants didn't pay directly for their own electricity, so the hall light was on the same line as the foyer of apartment A on every floor. They must have blown a fuse once, and she'd noticed that.

But why? What was she trying for?

The telephone call, as he was leaving the house. Somehow or other, she'd worked it out, and she knew that Levine was on his way here, that Levine knew the truth.

He backed away toward the doorway. He needed to get to the elevator, to get down and away from here. He'd call the precinct. They'd need flashlights, and numbers. This darkness was no place for him, alone.

A face rose toward him, luminous, staring, grotesque, limned in pale cold green, a staring devil face shining in green fire against the blackness. He cried out, instinctive panic filling his mouth with bile, and stumbled backwards away from the thing, bumping painfully into the doorpost. And the face disappeared.

He felt around him, his hands shaking, all sense of direction lost. He had to get out, he had to find the door. She was trying to kill him, she knew he knew and she was trying to kill him the same way she'd killed Walker. Trying to stop his heart.

A shriek jolted into his ears, loud, loud, incredibly loud, magnified far beyond the power of the human voice, a world-filling scream of hatred, grating him to the bone, and his flailing hands touched a wall, he leaned against it trembling. His mouth was open, straining for air, his chest was clogged, his heart beat fitfully, like the random motions of a wounded animal. The echoes of the shriek faded away, and then it sounded again, even louder, all around him, vibrating him like a fly on a pin.

He pushed away from the wall, blind and panic-stricken, wanting only to get away, to be away, out of this horror, and he stumbled into an armchair, lost his balance, fell heavily forward over the chair and rolled to the floor.

He lay there, gasping, unthinking, as brainlessly terrified as a rabbit in a trapper's snare. Pinwheels of light circled the corners of his stinging eyes, every straining breath was a searing fire in his throat. He lay on his back, encumbered and helpless in the heavy overcoat, arms and legs curled upward in feeble defense, and waited for the final blow.

But it didn't come. The silence lengthened, the blackness of the apartment remained unbroken, and gradually rationality came back to him and he could close his mouth, painfully swallow saliva, lower his arms and legs, and listen.

Nothing. No sound.

She'd heard him fall, that was it. And now she was waiting, to be sure he was dead. If she heard him move again, she'd hurl another thunderbolt, but for now she was simply waiting.

And the wait gave him his only chance. The face had been only phosphorescent paint on a balloon, pricked with a pin when he cried out. The shriek had come, most likely, from a tape recorder. Nothing that could kill him, nothing that could injure him, if only he kept in his mind what they were, and what she was trying to do.

My heart is weak, he thought, *but not that weak. Not as weak as Walker's, still recovering from his first attack. It could kill Walker, but it couldn't quite kill me.*

He lay there, recuperating, calming, coming back to himself. And then the flashlight flicked on, and the beam was aimed full upon him.

He raised his head, looked into the light. He could see nothing behind it. "No, Amy," he said. "It didn't work."

The light flicked off.

"Don't waste your time," he said into the darkness. "If it didn't work at first, when I wasn't ready for it, it won't work at all.

"Your mother is dead," he said, speaking softly, knowing she was listening, that so long as she listened she wouldn't move. He raised himself slowly to a sitting position. "You killed her, too. Your father and mother both. And when you called my home, to tell me that she'd killed herself, and my wife told you I'd already left, you knew then that I knew. And you had to kill me, too. I'd told you that my heart was weak, like your father's. So you'd kill me, and it would simply be another heart failure, brought on by the sight of your mother's corpse."

The silence was deep and complete, like a forest pool. Levine shifted, gaining his knees, moving cautiously and without sound.

"Do you want to know how I knew?" he asked her. "Monday in Civics Miss Haskell told you about the duties of the police. But Miss Haskell told me that you were always at least a month ahead in your studies. Two weeks before your stepfather died, you read that assignment in your schoolbook, and then and there you decided how to kill them both."

He reached out his hand, cautiously, touched the chair he'd tripped over, shifted his weight that way, and came slowly to his feet, still talking. "The only thing I don't understand," he said, "is why. You steal books from the library that they won't let you read. Was this the same thing to you? Is it all it was?"

From across the room, she spoke, for the first time. "You'll never understand, Mr. Levine," she said. That young voice, so cold and adult and emotionless, speaking out contemptuously to him in the dark.

And all at once he could *see* the way it had been with Walker. Somnolent in the bed, listening to the frail fluttering of the weary heart, as Levine often lay at night, listening and wondering. And suddenly that shriek, out of the midafternoon stillness, coming from nowhere and everywhere, driving in at him—

Levine shivered. "No," he said. "It's you who don't understand. To steal a book, to snuff out a life, to you they're both the same. You don't understand at all."

She spoke again, the same cold contempt still in her voice. "It was bad enough when it was only *her*. Don't do this, don't do that. But then she had to marry him, and there were two of them watching me all the time, saying no no no, that's all they ever said. The only time I could ever have some peace was when I was at my grandmother's."

"Is *that* why?" He could hear again the baby crying, the gigantic ego of the very young, the imperious demand that *they* be attended to. And in the place of terror, he now felt only rage. That this useless half-begun thing should kill, and kill—

"Do you know what's going to happen to you?" he asked her. "They won't execute you, you're too young. They'll judge you insane, and they'll lock you away. And there'll be guards and matrons there, to say don't do this and don't do that, a million million times more than you can imagine. And they'll keep you locked away in a little room, forever and ever, and they'll let you do *nothing* you want to do, *nothing*."

He moved now, feeling his way around the chair, reaching out to touch the wall, working his way carefully toward the door. "There's nothing you can do to me now," he said. "Your bag of tricks won't work, and I won't drink the poison you fed your mother. And no one will believe the suicide confession you forged. I'm going to phone the precinct, and they'll come and get you, and you'll be locked away in that tiny room, forever and ever."

The flashlight hit the floor with a muffled thud, and

then he heard her running, away from him, deeper into the apartment. He crossed the room with cautious haste, hands out before him, and felt around on the floor till his fingers blundered into the flashlight. He picked it up, clicked it on, and followed.

He found her in her mother's bedroom, standing on the window sill. The window was wide open, and the December wind keened into the room. The dead woman lay reposed on the bed, the suicide note conspicuous on the nightstand. He shone the light full on the girl, and she warned him, "Stay away. Stay away from me."

He walked toward her. "They'll lock you away," he said. "In a tiny, tiny room."

"No, they won't!" And she was gone from the window.

Levine breathed, knowing what he had done, that he had made it end this way. She hadn't ever understood death, and so it was possible for her to throw herself into it. The parents begin the child, and the child ends the parents. A white rage flamed in him at the thought.

He stepped to the window and looked down at the broken doll on the sidewalk far below. In another apartment, above his head, a baby wailed, creasing the night. *Make way, make way.*

He looked up. "We will," he whispered. "We will. But in our own time. Don't rush us."

STORM IN THE CHANNEL
by Georges Simenon

I

It looked as if fate had taken advantage of Maigret's recent retirement to confront him, ironically, with the most glaring proof of the unreliability of human evidence. And this time the famous Superintendent, or rather the man who had borne that title only three months earlier, was on the wrong side of the counter, so to speak, facing a policeman's searching gaze and being asked the question:

'Are you sure it was half-past six, or a little earlier, and that you were sitting beside the fire?'

Now Maigret realised with appalling clarity how a small handful of human beings, half a dozen in this case, were suddenly going to be paralysed by this simple question:

'What exactly were you doing between six and seven o'clock?'

If only it had been a question of disorderly, or dramatic, or tragic incidents! But it was nothing of the sort; merely a matter of half a dozen people hanging about, waiting for dinner on a wet night in the two or three public sitting-rooms of a boarding-house!

And Maigret, when he was questioned, hesitated like a forgetful schoolboy or a false witness.

'A net weight' is putting it mildly. At the Gare Saint-Lazare there had been a notice: 'Storm in the Channel. The Dieppe-Newhaven crossing may be delayed.'

And a good many English travellers turned around and went back to their hotels.

At Dieppe, in the main street, it looked as if the

wind would tear down the street signs. You had to lean against the street doors to open them. The water came down in bucketfuls, with a noise like waves crashing on shingle. Sometimes a figure would dart past, someone who had to go out, clinging close to the walls, his head covered with a coat.

It was November. The lights had had to be put on at four o'clock. At the harbour station, the boat which should have left at two lay alongside the fishing-smacks whose masts were clashing together.

Madame Maigret had resignedly fetched from her room a piece of knitting which she had started in the train. She was sitting close to the stove, while an unfamiliar ginger cat, the boarding-house cat, had come to nestle in her lap.

From time to time she raised her head and cast a woebegone glance at Maigret, who was wandering about like a lost soul.

'We ought to have gone to the hotel,' she sighed. 'You'd have found someone there to play cards with.'

Obviously! But Madame Maigret, ever thrifty, had got from some friend or other the address of this godforsaken boarding-house at the end of the quay, amid the gloomy desolation of the summer visitors' district, where in winter all the shutters were closed and all the doors barred.

And yet this was supposed to be a holiday trip, the first, really, that the pair of them had taken since their honeymoon.

Maigret was free at last! He had left the Quai des Orfèvres and he could go to bed at night secure in the knowledge that he would not be disturbed by a telephone call summoning him to examine a corpse that was not yet cold.

And so, as Madame Maigret had long wanted to

visit England, he had made up his mind:

'We'll go and spend a fortnight in London. I'll take the opportunity to look up some of my colleagues at Scotland Yard with whom I worked during the war.'

Just their luck! A storm in the Channel, the boat delayed, and this gloomy boarding-house, remembered on the spur of the moment by Madame Maigret, its very walls exuding meanness and boredom!

The landlady, Mademoiselle Otard, was a spinster of fifty who tried to disguise her sourness behind honeyed smiles. Her nostrils twitched involuntarily every time she came across the trail of tobacco-smoke that followed Maigret in his wanderings to and fro. Several times she had been on the point of commencing that it was not the thing to smoke a pipe incessantly in small overheated rooms where ladies were sitting. On these occasions Maigret, feeling a row imminent, looked her in the eyes so calmly that she preferred to turn her head away.

She was equally disgusted when she saw the Superintendent, who had never been able to break himself of the habit, hovering about the stoves, then seizing the poker and raking the coal so energetically that the chimneys roared like furnaces.

The house was not a large one. It was a two-storey villa converted into a boarding-house. There was a passage by way of entrance hall, but for economy's sake it was rarely lighted, nor was the staircase leading to the first and second floors, so that every now and then you would hear people stumbling up the stairs, or a hand groping for the door-knob.

The front room served as a lounge, with funny little armchairs of greenish velvet and tattered old magazines on the table.

Then there was the dining-room, where guests were

also allowed to sit except at meal-times.

Madame Maigret was in the lounge. Maigret wandered from one room to the other, from one stove to the other, from one poker to the other.

At the back was the pantry where Irma, the fifteen-year-old maid, was busy that afternoon cleaning knives and plate with silver polish.

And finally there was the kitchen, the domain of Mademoiselle Otard and of Jeanne, the older of the two maids, a slattern in her late twenties, perpetually slipshod, unkempt and of dubious cleanliness, and moreover perpetually embittered, looking about her resentfully and suspiciously.

The only other member of the household was a bewildered little boy of four who was always being pushed around, scolded and slapped: Jeanne's son, as Maigret learned by questioning the younger servant.

Elsewhere, in such weather, time might not have passed very cheerfully. Here it dragged funereally, and there must have been far more seconds to the minute here than anywhere else, for the hands seemed not to move at all on the face of the black marble clock standing under its glass case on the mantelpiece.

'Try to take advantage of a lull to go to the café. You're bound to find someone there to have a game with,' suggested Madame Maigret.

One couldn't even have a quiet chat in the place, for there was always somebody about. Mademoiselle Otard bustled from kitchen to lounge, opening drawers or cupboards, sitting down, going off again as if she had to keep an eye on everyone or a disaster would happen. As though if she stayed away for a quarter of an hour somebody would take the opportunity to pinch her old copies of *La Mode du Jour* or set fire to the sideboard!

From time to time Irma came in too, to put away

knives, spoons and forks in that same sideboard and take others out.

As for the sad lady, as the Maigrets called her because they did not know her name, she sat bolt upright on a chair beside the dining-room stove, reading a book whose title could not be seen because it had lost its cover.

As far as they could discover, she had been there for several weeks. She seemed to be about thirty, and in poor health; perhaps she had come to convalesce after some operation? At any rate she moved about with the utmost caution, as if she were afraid of damaging herself. She ate little, and always sighed as she ate, doubtless regretting the minutes wasted in such a vulgar activity.

As for the other lady, the young bride as Maigret called her with a sardonic smile, she was quite the reverse, and she was forever making a draught as she swept from one armchair to another.

The 'young bride' was probably in her early forties. She was short and stout and definitely not easy-going; the proof was that her husband came hurrying up at her slightest summons, assuming beforehand an obedient, sheepish air.

This husband was about thirty, and it was obvious from a glance that he had not married for love but had sacrificed his freedom in order to ensure for himself a comfortable old age.

Their name was Mosselet: Jules and Emilie Mosselet.

Though the clock hands did not move fast, they must have moved a bit, for Maigret remembered afterwards having looked at the time when Jeanne brought the sad lady a peppermint tisane; it was a few minutes past five, and Jeanne was looking surlier than ever.

It was shortly after this that the young Englishman, Mr. John, came in from outside, letting the cold wind and the rain into the house and bringing trickles of water into the lounge off his dripping raincoat.

He looked flushed with the keen air and the news he was bringing. He announced in a strong English accent:

'The boat's going to sail . . . My luggage can be taken out, Mademoiselle.'

He had been restless ever since the morning, for he was eager to get back to England, and now he had just come from the harbour station where he had learnt that the Channel steamer was going to attempt the crossing.

'Have you got my bill ready?'

Maigret hesitated for a moment. He was on the point of following his wife's advice, at the risk of a soaking, and running down the street as far as the Brasserie des Suisses, where at least there would be some life and activity.

He even went as far as the coat-stand in the hall, and noticed in the semi-darkness the Englishman's three big suitcases. Then he shrugged his shoulders and went into the lounge.

'Why don't you go? You're just getting irritable unnecessarily,' said Madame Maigret.

This remark was enough to make him subside heavily into an armchair, pick up the first magazine he saw and begin to turn over its pages.

The remarkable thing was that he had strictly nothing to do and nothing to preoccupy him. Logically, he should have been in a state of perfect relaxation.

The house was not large. From any point in it you could hear the slightest sounds; in fact in the evening, when the Mosselet couple retired to their bedroom, it became quite embarrassing.

But Maigret saw nothing, heard nothing, had not the faintest presentiment.

He was vaguely aware of Mr. John paying his bill

and going into the pantry to tip Irma. He made some vague reply to the Englishman's vague goodbye and realized that Jeanne, being heftier than the young man, was going to carry two of the cases to the boat.

But he did not see her go. It didn't interest him. He happened to be reading a long article in tiny print on the habits of field-mice—the magazine he had picked up at random being an agricultural journal—and he had ended up by becoming absurdly fascinated by it.

After that, the minute hand could creep forward on the grey-green clock-face without anybody noticing. Madame Maigret, counting the stitches in her knitting, was moving her lips in silence. From time to time a lump of coal crackled in one of the stoves or a gust of wind howled in the chimney.

The clink of china indicated that Irma was laying the table. There was a vague smell of frying that heralded the traditional evening dish of whiting.

And suddenly voices rang out in the night, excited voices that seemed to spring from the storm itself and that drew nearer, sounded right up against the shutters, stopped at the door and were brought to a noisy close by the most violent ring of the bell ever heard in that house.

Even then Maigret did not give a start. For hours he had been longing for a break in the day's monotony. Now that it had come, far more sensational than anything he could have expected, he sat absorbed in stories about field-mice.

'Yes, this is the house . . .' Mademoiselle Otard's voice was heard saying.

She ushered in air and wetness and damp clothes, and red excited faces. Maigret was obliged to raise his head. He caught sight of a policeman's uniform and the black overcoat of a little man with an unlighted cigar in his mouth.

'I think this is where a certain Jeanne Fénard was in service?' said the man with the cigar.

Maigret noticed that the little boy was there, having crept in from heaven knows where, probably from the depths of the kitchen.

'She has just been shot dead with a revolver as she was going along the Rue de la Digue.'

Mademoiselle Otard's immediate reaction was one of incredulity and suspicion. She was patently not the sort of person to be taken in easily and, tight-lipped, she let fall the magnificent comment:

'Really?'

But the sequel left her in no doubt, for the man with the unlighted cigar went on:

'I am the police inspector. I want you to come with me to identify the body . . . And I want nobody else to leave the house.'

Maigret's eyes were twinkling mischievously. His wife looked at him as if to say:

'Why don't you tell them who you are?'

But Maigret had retired such a short time ago that he was still savouring the delights of anonymity. He sank back into his armchair with real enjoyment. He scrutinized the inspector with a critical eye.

'Kindly put on your coat and follow me . . .'

'Where to?' Mademoiselle Otard protested again.

'To the morgue . . .'

There followed loud screams, a genuine or else a well-simulated fit of hysterics, with a moan from the sad lady visitor, whom Maigret had forgotten.

Irma darted in from her pantry, holding a plate in her hand.

'Is Jeanne dead?'

'It's none of your business,' declared Mademoiselle Otard. 'I shall be back presently. You can serve dinner in the meantime.'

She glanced at the little boy, who had not understood what was going on and was wandering about among the grown-ups' legs.

'Shut him up in his room . . . Put him to bed.'

Where was Madame Mosselet at that moment? The question would seem an easy one and yet Maigret couldn't have answered it. On the other hand Mosselet, who wore ridiculous red felt slippers indoors, was standing there somewhere near the hall. He must have heard the noise from his room and come down.

'What's happening?' he asked.

But the local inspector was in a hurry. He said a few words in a whisper to the uniformed policeman, who took off his cape and cap and settled down by the fire, like someone who has come to stay.

Meanwhile Mademoiselle Otard was being hurried out, wearing a yellow waterproof coat and rubber boots. She turned round once more to call out to Irma:

'Hurry up and serve dinner! The fish'll be burnt!'

Irma was weeping mechanically, as though out of politeness, because somebody had died. She wept as she handed round the dishes, turning her head away so that her tears should not fall into the food.

Here, Maigret noticed that Madame Mosselet was at table, showing no other emotion than curiosity.

'I wonder how it can have happened . . . Was it in the street? . . . Are there gangsters in Dieppe?'

Maigret was eating hungrily. Madame Maigret could not understand how her husband could seem so uninterested in this affair, when his whole life had been spent investigating crimes.

The sad lady was staring at her whiting and the

whiting was staring back at her. From time to time she opened her mouth, not to eat but to breathe out a little air by way of a sigh.

As for the policeman, he had taken a chair and was sitting astride it, watching the others eat and longing for a chance to show off.

'It was I that found her,' he said with pride to Madame Mosselet, who seemed the most interested.

'How?'

'Quite by chance . . . I live in the Rue de la Digue, a little street that runs from the quay to the far end of the harbour, beyond the tobacco factory. That's as good as saying that nobody ever goes down it. I was walking fast with my head bent and I saw something dark . . .'

'How dreadful!' said Madame Mosselet, without conviction.

'At first I thought it might be a drunk, for there's always some of them lying about the pavement . . .'

'Even in winter?'

'Particularly in winter, because people begin drinking to get warm . . .'

'While in summer they drink to get cool!' Jules Mosselet said jokingly, with a sly glance at his wife.

'That's about it . . . I touched the body . . . I found it was a woman . . . I called for help, and when she had been carried into a pharmacy, the one on the corner of the Rue de Paris, we saw that she was dead . . . And that was when I recognized her, because I know all the faces in the neighbourhood. I told the Chief: "That's the maid from the Pension Otard . . ." '

Then Maigret inquired hesitantly, as if reluctant to interfere in what did not concern him:

'Were there any suitcases beside her?'

'Why should there have been suitcases?'

'I don't know . . . I wonder, too, if she was facing

towards the harbour or in this direction . . .'

The policeman scratched his head.

'Wait a minute...I believe, the way she was lying, she must have been coming this way when it happened.'

He hesitated a moment, then made up his mind to take hold of the bottle of red wine and pour himself a glass, murmuring:

'May I?'

This action had brought him close to the table. There were still two whiting lying flat on the dish. He hesitated once more, took one of them, ate it without knife or fork and went over to throw the backbone into the coal scuttle.

Then he looked questioningly round the table, made sure that nobody wanted the second whiting and ate it like the first, took another drink and sighed:

'It must have been a crime of passion . . . That girl was a really fast one. She was always hanging around the dance-hall at the far end of the harbour . . .'

'Well, that makes it different,' murmured Madame Mosselet, who seemed to think that if passion was involved the whole thing was quite natural.

'What surprises me,' went on the policeman, while Maigret never took his eyes off him, 'is that it was done with a gun. Sailors, you know, are more likely to use knives.'

At that moment Mademoiselle Otard reappeared, and the wind, which had given a flush to other people's faces, had made hers pale. The incident, moreover, had given her a sense of her own importance, and her whole attitude proclaimed:

'I know certain things, but don't expect me to tell you . . .'

Her glance swept round the table, the diners and their plates, taking stock of the fish-bones. She said se-

verely to Irma, who stood glued to the doorway, snivel-
ling:

'Why don't you get on with serving the veal?'

Finally she turned to the policeman:

'I hope they've given you something to drink? . . .
Your chief will be here in a few minutes. He's telephon-
ing to Newhaven.'

Maigret gave a start and she noticed it. It struck her
as odd, and an obvious look of suspicion crossed her face.
Consequently she felt bound to add:

'At least I suppose so . . .'

She did not suppose so; she knew. So the local inspector had heard about Mr. John and his hurried depar-
ture.

For the time being, then, the official line followed
the trail of the young Englishman.

'All this is going to make me ill again!' the sad lady
murmured plaintively. She opened her lips scarcely three
times a day except to sigh.

'And what about me?' asked Mademoiselle Otard
indignantly, for she could not endure that anyone else
should be more affected by the event than herself. 'You
think this is going to be convenient for me? A girl I spent
months training after a fashion . . . Irma! When are you
going to bring that gravy?'

The most obvious result of these comings and goings
was to let wafts of cold air into the house; instead of
merging in the surrounding warmth, it formed little fluttering draughts that crept round the back of your neck
and aroused a shiver between your shoulder blades.

So much so that Maigret got up and, disregarding
the empty coal scuttle, went to poke the stove. Then he
filled his pipe, lit it with a paper spill held close to the
flame and automatically took up his favourite attitude, in
which Headquarters at the Quai des Orfévres had so

often seen him, pipe between his teeth, back to the fire, hands clasped behind his back, with that indefinable air of stubbornness that he assumed when apparently unrelated facts began to group themselves in his mind and form, as it were, a still unsubstantial germ of truth.

The arrival of the Dieppe inspector did not rouse him from his immobility. He heard:

'The boat hasn't got there yet . . . They're going to let me know . . .'

And one could readily imagine the steamer tossed in the darkness of the Channel, where nothing could be seen but the pale crests of huge waves. And the seasick passengers, the deserted buffet, anxious shadows on the darkened deck, with no other guide than the flash of the Newhaven lighthouse.

'I shall be obliged to question all of these ladies and gentlemen in turn,' said the inspector.

Mademoiselle Otard understood and decided:

'We can shut the communicating doors. You can sit in the lounge and...'

The inspector had had no dinner, but there were no more whiting left on the table and he did not like to thrust his fingers into the dish where slices of veal were congealing.

II

It happened by chance. The policeman had looked round to decide whom he should begin with. His glance had met that of Madame Maigret, who seemed calm enough to set an example.

'Come in,' he had said to her, opening the door of

the lounge and then closing it behind her, while a faint smile flitted across the lips of the former Superintendent her husband.

Although the door was shut you could hear practically everything that was being said on the other side, and Maigret's smile grew more marked when his colleague in the next room asked:

'Spelt *ai* or *é*?'

'*Ai.*'

'Like the famous detective?'

And the admirable wife merely replied:

'Yes!'

'You're not related to him?'

'I'm his wife.'

'But then . . . In that case . . . It's your husband who's here with you?'

And a minute later Maigret was in the lounge, facing the little fellow who looked radiant and at the same time a trifle anxious.

'Now admit that you were trying to have me on! . . . When I think that I was going to question you like all the rest . . . I must point out that what I'm doing now is just to carry out normal procedure and also in a way to kill time till I get news from Newhaven . . . But you were on the spot. You must have seen the whole thing coming in a way—surely you've got more definite ideas and I'd be grateful if you . . .'

'I assure you that I haven't the slightest idea.'

'Well, who knew that the murdered girl was going out?'

'The people in the house, of course. But this is where I realize how hard it is to be a witness; I'm quite incapable of stating definitely who was in the house at that moment.'

'You were busy?'

'I was reading . . .'

He did not care to add that he had been reading an article on the life of moles and field-mice.

'I was vaguely aware of noise and bustle... Then ...'

'Madame Mosselet, for instance! Was she downstairs or wasn't she? And if she was, which room was she in? What was she doing?'

The Dieppe inspector was not satisfied. He was almost convinced that his illustrious colleague was enjoying letting him struggle on his own, and no doubt he promised himself secretly to show Maigret how he, a provincial detective, could conduct an inquiry.

The sad lady was sent for; her name was Germaine Moulineau and she was a schoolteacher on convalescent leave.

'I was in the dining-room,' she mumbled. 'I remember thinking it was unfair to let that poor girl carry the Englishman's cases when there were strong men sitting about killing time.'

This was aimed at Maigret, as was proved by the glance she cast at his broad shoulders when she referred to 'strong men'.

'After that you didn't leave the dining-room?'

'I went up to my bedroom.'

'Did you stay there long?'

'About a quarter of an hour . . . I took a tablet and waited for it to take effect . . .'

'Forgive the question I'm going to ask you, but I'm asking all the guests in the house the same thing and I consider it a mere formality. I suppose you have not been out today, so that your clothes must be dry?'

'No . . . About the middle of the afternoon I went out for a moment.'

Yet another proof of the unreliability of evidence! Maigret had not noticed that she had gone out, nor that she had left the dining-room for a quarter of an hour.

'Perhaps you went to the chemist's to fetch your tablets?'

'No . . . I wanted to look at the harbour in the wind and rain . . .'

'Thank you...Next, please!'

The next was Irma, the young maid, still sniffling and crumpling the corner of her apron between her fingers.

'Do you know if your friend Jeanne had any enemies?'

"No, Monsieur.'

'Had you noticed any change in her behaviour, suggesting that she was afraid because of some threat?'

'Only that she told me this morning she wasn't going to stick in this hole much longer. That's what she said . . .'

'You're not treated well here?'

'I didn't say that,' Irma declared hastily, with a glance at the door.

'Well, then, do you know if Jeanne had any lovers?'

'She must have done.'

'Why'd you say she must have done?'

'Because she was always afraid of having a baby.'

'Do you know any of their names?'

'There was one fisherman who sometimes came and whistled in the alley, a chap called Gustave . . .'

'What alley's that?'

'The alley behind the house. You can get out that way, across the courtyard behind the kitchen.'

'Did you go out this evening?'

She hesitated, nearly said no, hesitated again and then admitted:

'Just for a second. I went to the baker's to get a croissant.'

'What time was that?'

'I don't know . . . I suppose about five.'

'Why did you have to get a croissant?'

'We don't get a lot to eat,' she muttered in a barely audible voice.

'Thank you.'

'You won't tell on me?'

'You needn't worry . . . Next, please! . . .'

This time Jules Mosselet made his appearance, looking completely self-possessed.

'All yours, Inspector!'

'Did you go out this afternoon?'

'Yes, Inspector . . . I went to get some cigarettes.'

'At what time?'

'It must have been five or ten minutes to five . . . I came back almost immediately. The weather was shocking.'

'You didn't know the dead woman?'

'I didn't know her at all, Inspector.'

He was thanked, as the others had been, and his wife took his place and was asked the question that had now become a ritual:

'Did you go out this afternoon?'

'I suppose I've got to answer?'

'You'd be well advised to do so.'

'In that case I only beg you not to mention it to Jules. You'll see why. He's very attractive to women and because he's a weak character, I don't trust him. When I heard him go out I followed him to find out where he was going . . .'

'And where did he go?' asked the Inspector with a wink at Maigret.

The answer was somewhat unexpected.

'I don't know . . .'

'What d'you mean, you don't know? You've just admitted that you followed him . . .'

'That's just it! I thought I was following him. Don't you understand? By the time I had put on my coat and opened my umbrella he had already got to the corner of the first street. And when I got there myself I saw a figure in a brown raincoat in the distance and I followed it. It wasn't until five minutes later, when the person went past a lighted shop window, that I realized it wasn't Jules . . . So I came back and behaved as if nothing had happened . . .'

'How long after you did he come back?'

'I don't know . . . I was upstairs. He may have stayed downstairs for a while.'

Just then there was a sharp ring of the bell and a policeman in uniform handed a note to the inspector, who opened it and presently handed it over to Maigret:

Nobody answering to the name or description of John Miller landed from the Dieppe boat at Newhaven.

The police inspector had politely invited Maigret to accompany him on his investigation if he was interested, but did not seem particularly enthusiastic, in view of his colleague's apparently unhelpful attitude.

However, as they walked together along the street, in constant danger of the tiles falling on their heads— there were broken pieces lying here and there on the pavement—he explained to Maigret:

'I don't want to leave anything to chance, as you'll have noticed. I shall be very surprised if there isn't something fishy about that John Miller. The landlady tells me he had been at her *pension* for several days, but that he had never given anything but evasive answers to her questions. He paid his bill in French money and—this is interesting—with an unusual quantity of small change. He went out very seldom, and only in the mornings. On two consecutive days Mademoiselle Otard met him in the market place, taking an apparent interest in butter, eggs and vegetables . . .'

'Or perhaps in the housewives' purses!' cut in Maigret.

'You think he's a pickpocket?'

'At any rate, that would explain how he might have got into England under a different name and in different clothes from those you had described to the English authorities.'

'That won't stop me from keeping on trying to get hold of him. And now we're going to Victor's, the café close to the fish market. I should like to meet that Gustave the little maid told us about, and to know whether he's the same as a certain Gustave Broken-Tooth with whom I've had a lot of dealings . . .'

'According to your man, the men hereabouts use knives rather than guns,' Maigret objected again, as he jumped over a deep puddle of water and got splashed nonetheless.

A few minutes later they went into Victor's, where the floor was thick with grease and a dozen or so tables were occupied by sailors in jerseys and clogs. The café was glaringly lit, and a juke-box was dispensing shrill music, while the proprietor and two slovenly waitresses bustled about.

It was obvious from the men's glances that they had recognized the local inspector, who went to sit with Maigret in a corner and ordered a beer. When one of the girls served him, he caught hold of her apron and asked her in a low voice:

'What time did Jeanne come in this afternoon?'

'What Jeanne?'

'Gustave's girl . . .'

The waitress hesitated, glanced at one of the groups of men, and then pondered:

'I don't think I saw her!' she said at last.

'She often comes, doesn't she?'

'Sometimes. But she doesn't come in. She opens the door a crack to see if he's there and, if he is, he goes to join her outside.'

'Did Gustave spend the evening here?'

'You'll have to ask my friend Berthe . . . I had to go out.'

Maigret was smiling to himself. He seemed delighted to find that he was not the only person who could not provide definite evidence.

Berthe was the other waitress. She squinted; possibly that was what gave her such a disagreeable air.

'If you want to know,' she told the inspector, 'you'll have to ask him yourself. I'm not paid to do police work.'

By now the first waitress had already spoken to a red-headed fellow in rubber boots, who stood up, hitched up his duck trousers, which were fastened with a piece of string, spat on the floor, walked up to the inspector and, when he opened his mouth, revealed a broken tooth right in the middle.

'Is it me you're talking about?'

'I want to know whether you've seen Jeanne this evening . . .'

'What's it got to do with you?'

'Jeanne is dead.'

'It's not true . . .'

'I tell you she's dead. She was shot dead in the street.'

The man was genuinely surprised. He looked round

at the others and shouted:

'Here, what's all this about? Is Jeanne really dead?'

'Answer my question. Did you see her?'

'Oh well, can't be helped. I'd sooner tell the truth. She came here . . .'

'At what time?'

'I don't know . . . I was playing for drinks with Big Joe.'

'Was it after five?'

'Must have been!'

'Did she come in?'

'I don't allow her to come into the cafés I go to. I saw her face in the doorway. I went and told her to leave me alone.'

'Why?'

'Because!'

The proprietor had stopped the juke-box and silence reigned in the room. The other customers were trying to overhear snatches of the conversation.

'Had you been quarrelling?'

Broken-Tooth shrugged his shoulders, like someone who knows he's going to have a hard time making himself understood.

'We had and we hadn't . . .'

'Explain yourself!'

'Let's say that I had my eye on another girl and she was jealous.'

'What other girl?'

'One who came to the dance-hall with Jeanne once . . .'

'What's her name?'

'I don't even know it…Well, can't be helped, if you really want to know…I've never even touched her, so I can't get into trouble for that, in spite of her age…It's the kid that works at the boarding-house with Jeanne...That's all! When Jeanne came, I just went outside and told her that if she didn't leave me alone I'd hit her.'

'And after that? You went straight back into the cafe?'

'Not right away. I went to watch the Newhaven boat leaving...I thought it might get into difficulties on account of the current....Are you going to arrest me?'

'Not yet...'

'You needn't stand on ceremony, you know! We're getting used to always taking the rap for other people...And so Jeanne's dead! I hope she didn't suffer?'

It was a strange sensation, for Maigret, to be there and to have nothing to do. He was not used to being merely a member of the public. He heard a voice that was not his own asking the questions, and he had to make an effort not to break in, approving or disapproving.

Sometimes a question was on the tip of his tongue and it was a real torment to have to keep silent.

'Are you coming along?' the inspector asked Maigret, as he stood up and laid some money on the table.

'Where are you going?'

'To the police station. I've got to make out my report. Afterwards, I might as well go to bed. There's nothing more I can do today . . .'

Out on the pavement, however, he murmured as he turned up the collar of his overcoat:

'Of course I shall put a man on to tail Broken-Tooth. That's my method, and I think it used to be yours too...It's a mistake to try to get immediate results at all costs; one only gets tired and flustered. Tomorrow I shall have to deal with the Public Prosecutor's lot.'

Maigret chose to part company with him under the

red light at the police station. There was nothing for him to do in the office where his colleague was going to settle down quietly to writing a meticulous report.

The wind had dropped a little, but the rain was still falling, seeming even wetter because it was falling vertically. Few people were passing in front of the shop windows, which were still lighted up.

As he always used to do when a case was starting badly, Maigret began by wasting time. He went to the Brasserie des Suisses and spent a quarter of an hour uninterestedly watching a game of backgammon at the next table.

His shoes had let in water and he felt he was catching a cold. That decided him, after finishing his glass of beer, to order a rum toddy that sent the blood racing to his head.

'Oh, well,' he sighed as he got up.

It was none of his business! It was rather sickening, but he had looked forward to his retirement for so long that he wasn't going to grumble now it had come.

Out of doors, at the end of the quay beyond the harbour station, which was deserted and lit only by a single arc-lamp, Maigret caught sight of a blur of violet light on the wet pavement and remembered a certain dance-hall that had been mentioned.

Without having really made up his mind to go there, and although he was still resolved to keep out of this business, he found himself in front of a garish facade, vulgarly painted and lit by coloured lamps. When he opened the door a waft of dance music hit him, but he was disappointed to find the place almost empty.

Two women were dancing together, two working girls probably, out to get their money's worth, and the three musicians were playing for them alone.

'By the way, what day is it?' he asked the proprietor as he sat down at the bar.

'Monday. Today, of course, we shan't get a big crowd. Here, it's chiefly Saturdays and Sundays, and a bit on Thursdays. There'll be a few couples presently, when the cinema shuts down, although in this weather . . . What'll you drink?'

'A toddy . . .'

Maigret regretted his choice on seeing his toddy concocted from an unknown brand of rum and water boiled in a dubious-looking kettle.

'You haven't been here before, have you? Are you passing through Dieppe?'

'Just passing through, yes . . .'

And the man, misinterpreting his intentions, explained:

'You know, you won't find anything of that kind here. You can dance with these young ladies and offer them a drink, but as for anything else, well . . . Specially today!'

'Because there's nobody here?'

'Not only that . . . Look, you see those kids dancing? D'you know why they're dancing?'

'No.'

'To get rid of the blues. A little while ago one of them was crying and the other sat staring straight in front of her. I stood them a drink to cheer them up . . . It's not very pleasant to hear suddenly that one of your friends has been killed . . .'

'Oh, has there been an accident?'

'There's been a crime! In a little street not a hundred meters from here. A servant girl was picked up with a bullet in her head . . .'

And Maigret reflected:

'And it never occurred to me to ask if she'd been

shot in the head or in the chest!'

Then he said aloud:

'So the shot was fired at close quarters?'

'Very close, I'd say. In this darkness and in such stormy weather it would have been hard to aim from as much as three steps away. All the same I'll bet it wasn't a local man. They're ready enough with their fists, of course. Every Saturday I have to chuck somebody out before they get to fighting. Look, ever since I heard about it I haven't felt quite myself . . .'

He poured himself a little drink, and smacked his lips.

'Would you like me to introduce you?'

Maigret did not refuse quickly enough, and the proprietor had already summoned the two girls with a friendly wave.

'This gentleman's feeling lonely and would like to offer you a drink . . . Come over here. You'll be more comfortable in this corner . . .'

He winked at Maigret, as though authorizing him to take a few liberties unseen.

'What shall I bring you? Hot toddies?'

'That'll do . . .'

It was awkward, Maigret couldn't think how to handle this. The two girls were scrutinizing him stealthily and trying to make conversation.

'Won't you dance?'

'I can't dance . . .'

'Wouldn't you like us to teach you?'

No! There were limits, after all! He couldn't see himself gliding about the floor under the amused gaze of the three-man band!

'Are you a commercial traveller?'

'Yes. I'm just passing through. The boss has just

told me that your friend . . . I mean, that there's been a tragedy . . .'

'She wasn't a friend of ours!' retorted one of the girls.

'Oh? I understood . . .'

'If she'd been a friend of ours we shouldn't be here! But we knew her, same as we know all the girls that come here. Now she's dead we don't want to say anything against her. It's quite sad enough without that . . .'

'Of course . . .'

He had to agree with them. Above all he had to wait patiently without scaring his companions.

'Was she not very respectable?' he ventured at last.

'That's putting it mildly . . .'

'Shut up, Marie! Now she's dead . . .'

A few customers appeared. One of the girls danced several times with strangers. Then Maigret caught sight of Gustave Broken-Tooth, dead drunk, leaning against the bar.

The drunken man stared at Maigret as though he were on the point of recognizing him, and Maigret anticipated an unpleasant scene. But nothing happened. The man was too tipsy to see anything clearly and the proprietor was only waiting for a chance to throw him out.

In exchange for the favour he had done Maigret by introducing him to a couple of local beauties, he expected him to stand a round of toddies every quarter of an hour.

Consequently when the former Superintendent left the place at one o'clock in the morning, he lurched through the doorway, had some difficulty in fastening his overcoat, and splashed in all the puddles.

He forgot that the boarding-house guests who came in after eleven at night were supposed to ring a special bell which sounded in Mademoiselle Otard's room. He rang the front door bell violently, woke everybody up, and was given a most unfriendly welcome by the land-lady, who had thrown on a coat over her nightgown.

'Today of all days!' he heard her muttering.

Madame Maigret had gone to bed, but she switched on the light when she heard steps on the stairs and gazed in astonishment at her husband, who seemed to be walk-ing with exaggerated clumsiness and who tore off his col-lar with unwonted violence.

'Where on earth have you been?' she murmured, turning over towards the wall.

And he echoed her:

'Where have I been?'

Then he repeated, with a peculiar smile:

'Where have I been? . . . Supposing I've been to Villecomtois?"

She frowned, searched her memory, and felt sure she had never heard the name before.

'Is that near here?'

'It's in the Cher . . . Villecomtois!'

Better wait till next morning before bothering him with questions, she thought.

III

Whether at home or on her travels, whether she had gone to bed early or late (which seldom happened), Madame Maigret had a mania for getting up at an impos-sibly early hour. Maigret had already had an argument with her on the subject the day before, when he found her up and dressed at seven o'clock in the morning with nothing to do.

'I can't get used to staying in bed,' she had replied.

'I always feel I've got the housework to do.'

And the same thing happened that morning. He opened an eye, at one moment, because the yellow glare of the electric light was shining into it. It was not yet daylight and already his wife was making timid splashing noises in the room.

'What was that name?' Maigret wondered, half a-sleep, realizing to his annoyance that he was getting a headache.

The name he had triumphantly announced to his wife the night before, the name of some village or small town, had obsessed him so much that, as often happens, he had forgotten it by dint of thinking of it.

He thought he had only half fallen asleep, for he was still conscious of certain small facts; thus he noticed that the electric light had been switched off and that a bleary daylight replaced it. Then he heard an alarm clock ring somewhere in the house, somebody's footsteps on the stairs and the front door bell ringing twice.

He would have liked to know if it was still raining and whether the storm had died down, but he could not bring himself to open his mouth and ask. Then suddenly he sat up, for his wife was shaking him by the shoulder; it was broad daylight; his watch, on the bedside table, showed half past nine.

'What's up?'

'The local police inspector is downstairs . . .'

'What's that to do with me?'

'He's asking to see you . . .'

Of course, because the night before he had maybe drunk a toddy too many—and that quite unintentionally!—Madame Maigret felt bound to assume a protective and maternal air.

'Drink your coffee while it's hot . . .'

On such mornings it's always a bore getting dressed,

and Maigret almost put off the task of shaving to another day.

'What was the name I told you last night?' he asked.

'What name?'

'I mentioned a village . . .'

'Oh yes, I remember vaguely; it was somewhere in the Cantal . . .'

'No, no, in the Cher . . .'

'D'you think so? . . . I believe it ended in *on* . . .'

So she couldn't remember either! Well, it was no good worrying. He went downstairs still only half awake, his head heavy, and his pipe had not the same taste as on other mornings. He was surprised to find nobody in the kitchen or in the pantry; however, when he opened the dining-room door he discovered all the inmates of the house, sitting frozen into stillness as if for some ceremony, or to have a group photograph taken.

Mademoiselle Otard gave him a nasty reproachful look, doubtless because of his noisy entrance last night. The sad lady, in her armchair, was as remote as a dying woman who has lost touch with this world. As for the Mosselets, they must have quarrelled for the first time that day, for they avoided looking at each other and seemed to be blaming the whole world for their row.

Even little Irma was not the same, and seemed to have been steeped in vinegar.

'Good morning!' said Maigret, as cheerfully as possible.

Nobody answered, or made the slightest gesture in acknowledgement of his greeting. Meanwhile, however, the lounge door opened, and the police inspector, looking pleased with himself, held out his hand to his illustrious colleague.

'Please come in here . . . I had an idea I should find you still in bed . . .'

The door had closed again. They were alone in the lounge, where the fire had only just been lit and was still smoking. Through the window Maigret could see the grey quayside, still windswept, with clouds of spray flying from every big wave.

'Yes, I was tired,' he grunted.

And seeing the inspector's smile, he chose to show right away that he knew what the man was hinting at. He had not thought of one point last night, but now it recurred to him.

'Of course, your Gustave Broken-Tooth was there! So there was a policeman at his heels. And this policeman told you . . .'

'I assure you I had no intention of making the slightest reference to it . . .'

Idiot! So he thought that if Maigret had spent the evening at the dance-hall with those two girls, it was because . . .

'I've taken the liberty of disturbing you this morning because the Dieppe police have made a discovery which, if I may say so, is of a somewhat sensational character...'

Maigret poked the fire, out of habit. He would have liked a drink, something refreshing, lemon juice for instance.

'Didn't you notice anything when you came downstairs?' went on the inspector, who was in the seventh heaven, like an actor who has just been applauded tumultuously and who is about to deliver his best speech.

'Do you mean the people waiting in the dining-room?'

'Yes. I was anxious to get them all together in one room and prevent them from coming and going . . . I've got a piece of news which may perhaps surprise you: the man or woman who murdered Jeanne Fénard is one of them!'

It would have taken more than that to stir up Maigret on a morning like this, and he merely stared at his colleague with a heavy, almost listless gaze. And the local detective would have been greatly surprised if he had known that at that precise moment what was worrying Maigret was to remember the name of a village ending in *ois*.

'Look at this . . . Don't be afraid of touching it . . . The fingerprints, if there were any, have been washed away hours ago by the rain.'

This was a small card with which Maigret was already familiar, an oblong, greyish card bearing the printed word *Menu* surrounded by decorative scrolls.

The letters written in ink had been almost obliterated by the rain, but it was still possible to make out: Sorrel soup . . . Mackerel with mustard sauce . . .'

'That was the menu for the day before yesterday's dinner,' he commented, still showing no surprise.

'So I have just been told. One thing is certain, then: this is a menu from the Otard boarding-house, and a menu which was used the day before yesterday, namely the day before the crime. Let me tell you now that it was picked up this morning, by the merest chance, on the pavement in the Rue de la Digue, less than three metres away from the place where Jeanne was killed . . .'

'Evidently! . . .' grunted Maigret.

'You agree with me, don't you? You noticed that last night I was in no hurry to arrest Broken-Tooth, in spite of his past record, as some might have felt bound to do. My method, as I've told you, is not to hurry things at any price. The presence of this menu on the scene of the crime proves, in my opinion, that the murderer is staying in this house. And I'll go farther! In the midst of the storm that's still raging this morning, I tried to reconstruct his actions. Imagine that your hands are wet with rain and that you've got to shoot straight. What do you do? You take out your handkerchief and wipe your fingers. As he took out his handkerchief, the murderer dropped . . .'

'I understand . . .' sighed Maigret, lighting his second pipe of the day. 'And have you also worked out the meaning of the figures written on the back of the card?'

'Not yet, I must confess. Somebody who was here the night before last must have used this menu to make a note of something. I can read the pencilled figures: 79×140. And underneath that: 160×80. I thought at first that it might be the score of some game, but then I gave up that explanation. Nor can it be the time of a train or a boat, as had occurred to me. As far as that goes, the thing is still a complete mystery, but it is nonetheless evident that the murderer is one of the people in the boarding-house. That is why I have collected everybody in the dining-room under the eye of one of my officers. I wanted, before going any further, to ask you one question:

'Since you were here the night before last, did you at any time during the evening notice anybody using a pencil to make notes on a menu-card? . . .'

No! Maigret had noticed nothing of the sort. He remembered that Monsieur and Madame Mosselet had played draughts on a small table in the lounge, but he had already forgotten where the rest were. He himself had read the paper and gone to bed early.

'I think,' went on the inspector, pleased with his little sensation, 'that we can now examine our people one after the other.'

And Maigret was still hunting for that wretched

name, growing thirstier and thirstier, and sighing:

'Not until I've had something to drink, please!'

He opened the communicating door and saw Madame Maigret, who had virtuously come to sit with all the rest. In the grey light, the atmosphere was that of a small-town dentist's waiting room. They sat behind half-drawn curtains, with sullen faces, not daring to stretch out their legs, surreptitiously exchanging cautious or mistrustful glances.

Madame Maigret could obviously have avoided this ordeal. But it was just like her to want to behave like everybody else, to take her place in the line, having armed herself with her knitting, which kept her lips moving in silence as she counted her stitches.

Out of politeness, the inspector had brought her in first, had apologized for bothering her again, and had shown her the menu without attempting to catch her out.

'Does this remind you of anything?'

Madame Maigret glanced at her husband, shook her head, then reread the figures and frowned, as if reluctant to admit to a fantastic idea.

'Absolutely nothing!' she said at last.

'The evening before last, did you see anybody scribbling on a menu?'

'I must admit that as I never stopped knitting I didn't notice what was going on around me.'

While she was saying this she made a little sign to her husband. And he, realizing that she had something to add but that she would have liked to do so confidentially, said out loud nevertheless:

'What is it?'

She felt annoyed with him. She was always afraid of making a blunder. Now she blushed, feeling intimidated; she hunted for words and apologised profusely.

'I don't know . . . I'm very sorry . . . Perhaps I'm

wrong . . . But I immediately thought, when I saw those figures . . .'

Her husband sighed, reflecting that she was incorrigible in her touching humility!

'You'll probably laugh at me . . . A hundred and forty centimetres is the width of some dress materials. Eighty centimetres is the width of some others. And the first figure seventy-nine, is the length you'd need for a skirt . . .'

She felt quite proud as she caught a gleam in Maigret's eyes, and now she went on volubly:

'The first two numbers, 79 × 140, represent exactly the amount of material needed for, say, a pleated skirt. But you can't get all materials in that width. For stuff that's eighty centimetres wide you'd need double the length to get in the pleats . . . I don't know if I'm making myself clear . . .'

And turning to her husband, she exclaimed:

'D'you think it could have ended in *ard*?'

For she was still hunting for that wretched name which she blamed herself for having forgotten.

'Yes, that's one of my house menus. But I didn't write those figures.' Mademoiselle Otard replied to the inspector's questions. 'And I'd like to say that if my house is to be kept in a state of siege I shall be obliged to . . .'

'Please forgive me, Madame . . .'

'Mademoiselle!'

'Forgive me, Mademoiselle, and I will do my best to cut this state of siege, as you call it, as short as possible. But let me tell you that we are certain that the murderer is a guest in this house and that in the circumstances we are entitled to stay . . .'

'I'd like to know who!' she retorted.

'So should I, and I hope that it won't be long before

we find out. Meanwhile I have a few questions to ask you which did not occur to me during yesterday's upheaval. How long had the Fénard girl been in your service?'

'Six months!' Mademoiselle Otard replied, curtly and reluctantly.

'Will you kindly tell me how she came into your house?'

And the woman, perhaps because she felt Maigret's sardonic gaze on her, retorted:

'Like anybody else: through the door!'

'I didn't expect a wisecrack at a time like this. Did the Fénard girl come to you through an employment agency?'

'No!'

'She came on her own initiative?'

'Yes!'

'You didn't know her, did you?'

'I did!'

Deliberately, she now answered with only the barely essential syllables.

'Where did you know her?'

'At home.'

'Meaning?'

'She worked for some years at the Anneau d'Or, where I was cashier.'

'Is that a restaurant?'

'A hotel-restaurant.'

'Whereabouts?'

'I've told you; at home, in Villecomtois . . .'

Maigret had to restrain himself not to give a start. So that was the crucial name, rediscovered at last: Villecomtois, in the Cher! And at this point he forgot the promise he had made himself to stay in the background.

'Did Jeanne come from Villecomtois?' he asked.

'No. She just happened to turn up there, as a maid-of-all-work . . .'

'Had she a child then?'

She retorted contemptuously:

'That was seven years ago, and Ernest is four . . .'

'Seven years since when?'

'Since I left to settle down here.'

'But what about her?'

'I don't know . . .'

'If I understand you rightly, she stayed there after you had left?'

'I suppose so.'

'Thank you!' said Maigret in the threatening tone of a lawyer who has just been cross-examining a recalcitrant witness in court.

For form's sake, the Dieppe inspector added:

'So in fact, she turned up here this summer and you engaged her on recognizing a girl from your part of the world, or more exactly a girl whom you had known at home? I understand your action. And it was all the more generous in that, for one thing, this Jeanne had a child, and for another, her manners and her behaviour were not exactly in keeping with the reputation of your boarding-house . . .'

'I did what I could!' was all Mademoiselle Otard would say.

A minute later it was Mosselet's turn to come in, a cigarette between his lips, his expression sly and condescending.

'Still at it?' he asked, perching on the corner of the table. 'You must admit that for a honeymoon trip . . .'

'Did you write this?'

He turned the menu over and over between his fingers, and inquired:

'Why should I be drawing up menus?'

'I'm talking about the pencil notes on the back . . .'

'I hadn't noticed . . . Sorry . . . No! It wasn't me. What's this all about?"

'Oh, nothing . . . I suppose you didn't see anybody writing on one of the menu cards the evening before last?'

'I must admit that I wasn't watching . . .'

'And you didn't know Jeanne?'

Then Jules Mosselet raised his head and said simply: 'How d'you mean I didn't know her?'

'I mean you didn't know her before you came here?'

'I had seen her before.'

'In Dieppe?'

'No! At home . . .'

The name was going to recur! Maigret, although a silent actor in this scene, was as jubilant as though he had been its hero.

'Where is your home?'

'Villecomtois!'

'You are from Villecomtois? Do you still live there?'

'Of course!'

'And you knew Jeanne Fénard there?'

'Everybody knew her, seeing she was the maid at the Anneau d'Or. I knew Mademoiselle Otard too, when she was cashier there. And that was why, when we came through Dieppe, my wife and I, we thought we'd be better off staying with somebody from our own part of the world . . .'

'Your wife is from Villecomtois too?'

'From Herbemont, a village five miles away. Comes to the same thing! When you're travelling you may as well do a good turn to people you know . . . And so when Mademoiselle Moulineau was ill . . .'

Maigret had to turn his head away not to smile, and this movement, as he realized, offended the inspector, who could not understand it. So all the characters involved in this Dieppe affair were from Villecomtois, a remote village of which nobody had heard tell until now!

Maigret reflected:

'It's pretty sure that the friend who gave my wife this address must come from Villecomtois too!'

As for the local inspector, completely baffled, he tried to maintain his dignity as he mumbled:

'Thank you. I shall probably need you again. Please ask your wife to come in.'

As soon as Mosselet's back was turned, Maigret picked up from the table the menu which provided such crucial evidence, slipped it into his pocket and laid a finger on his lips as though to tell his colleague:

'Don't mention this to her . . .'

Madame Mosselet took her husband's place with the dignified air of a woman for whom the law holds no terrors.

'What is it now?' she asked.

The Dieppe detective, deprived of the menu card, was at a loss what to say. He began:

'Do you live at Villecomtois?'

'Villecomtois, in the Cher, yes. My father bought the Anneau d'Or hotel there. He died, and I was left on my own and needed a man to run the house, so I got married . . . We closed down for a week for our honeymoon, but if this sort of thing is going on . . .'

'Excuse me!' interrupted Maigret. 'You were married at Villecomtois?'

'Of course . . .'

'How far is it from the nearest large town?'

'It's forty-three kilometres from Bourges . . .'

'Was it at Bourges, then, that you bought your trousseau?'

She stared at him for a moment in amazement. She must have been wondering:

'What business is it of his?'

Then, with an imperceptible shrug, she replied:

'No! I'm going to buy my trousseau in Paris.'

'Oh! So you're going to finish your honeymoon in Paris?'

'We were going to start it there. But I wanted to see the sea. So did Jules. We had never seen the sea, either of us. If it hadn't been for the rate of exchange we might have gone on to London . . .'

'So you brought as little luggage as possible with you. I see your point . . . In Paris, you'll have plenty of time to fit yourself out . . .'

She could not understand why this man, who was as broad and solid as a wardrobe, insisted on talking about such futile things. And yet he went on, puffing gently at his pipe:

'It'll be particularly convenient since you've practically got a model's figure. I bet you're size twelve.'

'A biggish twelve. Only as I'm rather short I have to have my dresses taken up . . .'

'You don't make them yourself?'

'I've got a little dressmaker whose work is as good as anybody's, and who only charges . . .'

At last she was struck by the abnormal character of this interview, and stared at the two men; she saw Maigret smiling and the other, rather ill at ease, seeming to wash his hands of the business.

'But what's all this about?' she suddenly asked.

'How much material would you need, one metre forty wide, to make a skirt?'

She was unwilling to answer. She did not know whether to laugh or to be angry.

'For a single skirt-length, seventy-eight or seventy-nine centimetres, wouldn't you?'

'So what?'

'Nothing . . . Don't worry . . . Just an idea of mine . . . We were talking about dresses, my wife and I, and I said you'd be easier to dress than she is . . .'

'What else do you want to know?'

She was glancing towards the door, as if afraid that her husband might take advantage of her absence to be off on some escapade.

'You are absolutely free to leave . . . The inspector is much obliged to you.'

She went out, still uneasy and anxious, with the suspicious look of some women who are so convinced of human perfidy that they cannot imagine they've been told the truth, even by chance.

'Can I go into the town?'

'If you want to. . .'

When the door had closed again the inspector got up, intending to rush into the dining-room and order a policeman to follow her.

'What are you doing?' asked Maigret, going over to the stove which he had not poked for a long time.

'But I assume . . .'

'You assume what?'

'You're not going to tell me . . . Remember, she was the one who gave us the weakest evidence yesterday . . . According to her, she went out to follow her husband, but she asserts that she mistook a stranger's figure for his and, after following it, came home disappointed . . . All this business about dress materials . . .'

'Exactly!'

'Exactly what?'

'I tell you these notes on the menu card prove that

she is not guilty, that no woman in the house is guilty and that's why it's unnecessary to interview the "sad lady"—that's what my wife and I call the schoolteacher. Remember that a woman carries her own measurements in her head and knows the width of materials well enough not to need to note them down. If, on the other hand, she has asked a man to buy something of the sort for her, or if that man wants to give her a surprise . . .'

He pointed to the old copies of *La Mode du Jour* lying on the table.

'I'm willing to bet,' he said, 'that we should find in here the pattern that took Madame Mosselet's fancy. She and her husband must have discussed dress materials . . . The husband made notes, with the intention of making her a present. It's specially important for him to be nice to her because, as we've been told, she's got the money, that's to say the Anneau d'Or hotel. He was picked because she needed a man about the house . . . and also, no doubt, because Madame Mosselet belatedly developed some romantic feelings. But she must keep a tight hold on him. She watches him. He comes here to stay with an old acquaintance without suspecting that Mademoiselle Otard has taken in an unfortunate creature who also once lived at Villecomtois . . .'

It was still raining. Transparent drops chased one another down the panes. From time to time a black mackintosh went past on the pavement, hugging the wall.

'It's none of my business, is it?' went on Maigret. 'But I didn't get an entirely favourable report on this woman Jeanne from those girls last night. She wasn't a nice type of girl. She was cantankerous, embittered by her misfortunes. She hated men, blaming them for her downfall, and she always managed to make them pay. For she was one of the rare habituées of the dance-hall

who was willing to spend the rest of the night out . . .
Rum toddies may stupefy one, but not as much as you
seem to think . . .'

The other man felt ill at ease, remembering his behaviour that morning, his mocking, supercilious smile
when Maigret had appeared.

'You can see the course of events for your-
self . . . You'll discover that Jeanne, back home, was the
mistress of this Mosselet, who's quite nasty himself.
You'll find out that he was the father of her kid and that
she has had more cuffs from him than thousand-franc or
even hundred-franc notes . . . Then she suddenly sees
him turn up here with a wife rolling in money and jealous as a tigress . . . What does she do?'

'Blackmails him,' the local inspector sighed regret-
fully.

And Maigret lit a fresh pipe, his third, muttering:

'It's as simple as that. She blackmails him, and as
he's scared of losing not his love but his bread-and-
butter . . .'

At that moment he opened the dining-room door
and saw them all still sitting in their places, as if they
were at the dentist's.

'Come here, you!' he said in a changed voice to Jules
Mosselet, who was rolling a cigarette.

'But . . .'

'Come on, now!'

Then to the policeman, who was nearly six foot tall:

'You come in too . . .'

And finally he gave the local inspector a look which
meant:

'With that sort of fellow, you know . . .'

Mosselet was less bumptious than he had been earlier, and seemed almost ready to hold up his arms to

ward off blows.

Maigret was anxious to keep out of it. The women, on the other side of the door, jumped as they heard voices raised, vehement protests, and then strange bumping noises.

As for Maigret, he was looking out of the window. He was thinking that perhaps the Newhaven boat would leave at two. Then, by a curious association of ideas, he reflected that he'd have to go and have a look at Villecomtois one of these days.

When he felt a tap on the shoulder he did not even turn round.

'Is it okay?' he asked.

'He's confessed.'

Maigret was obliged to stay a minute longer looking out of the window so as not to let the local inspector see his smile.

Sometimes it's better not to seem too clever . . .

MURDER IN THE DARK
by Hugh Pentecost

Lieutenant Pascal of the Homicide Division stood in the doorway looking around at the total confusion that engulfed the room. It was the living-room of a two-room suite at the old Bransfield Hotel on lower Fifth Avenue. Fifty years ago the Bransfield had been the headquarters of New York's Social Registerites, but it had long since gone to seed. The high ceilings no longer suggested their original style and dignity. Modern plumbing and heating had introduced exposed pipes, painted a garish imitation of silver. The overstuffed furniture was old and worn. The curtains at the windows were made of a dreary, soot-streaked netting. The only picture on the walls, evidently hung there to conceal a place where the wallpaper was peeling, was a brownish, faded print of Rosa Bonheur's *Horse Fair*.

The confusion, however, was not indigenous to the Bransfield. It centered in the body of an old man lying on the floor. The white hair of the corpse was matted with blood, a silver flower vase on the carpet having been used to smash in a human skull.

The room was crowded with people. There was the bright young man from the D.A's office. There were two patrol-car cops. There were half a dozen members of Pascal's staff who had preceded him—fingerprint experts, photographers, a couple of leg men, and a police stenographer.

There were two other persons present. The first was a girl, with bright gold hair. Whatever her emotions might be at the moment were concealed by a pair of black glasses in harlequin-shaped frames. The second was a young man, about six feet tall, with a wiry build and blue eyes that had little wrinkles at the corners from much exposure to sunshine.

There was no doubt about his emotional state. He was boiling with anger. He glared at Pascal with an expression which said: "What new idiot is this?"

Lieutenant Pascal was a squarely built, swarthy man, his face prematurely lined in good-natured grooves. He wore his hat pushed back on his thick, curly hair. As he stood in the doorway he went through the somnambulistic routine of lighting a fresh cigarette from the stub of an old one. He looked for some place to dispose of the stub and finally walked over to an open window and tossed it out — a violation of a city ordinance.

One of the leg men came bustling over to him, notebook in hand. "Good morning, Lieutenant."

"Hi," Pascal said, his eyes still traveling around the room.

"The dead man is George Rawn," the leg man said. "Registered here yesterday from Oklahoma City, along with the young guy there. His name is Kelly Cotter, also from Oklahoma City. He has a room down the hall. The old man was killed with that flower vase. He's been dead quite a while. We can't tell how long yet. Medical examiner hasn't showed. This Kelly Cotter reported the killing. Claims he came in here at nine-thirty and found the old man dead and that girl in here with the body. She's Carla Van Rooten. She's a wholesale diamond importer, offices on Fifth Avenue. Lives in a duplex apartment with a maiden aunt over on East End Avenue."

Pascal was listening, but he was also looking. He saw the empty whiskey bottle on the table and the two tumblers standing beside it. He saw clothes and luggage scattered around the room. He saw sofa cushions on the floor. He saw that the seat of an overstuffed armchair had been ripped open and the stuffing pulled out.

"What have you been looking for?" Pascal asked.

"*We* haven't been looking for anything yet," the leg man said. "That was the murderer. He—or she—was looking for more than a hundred thousand dollars' worth of rough diamonds."

"Diamonds? Belong to whom?"

"The old man," the leg man said. "That's why he was killed, as near as we can figure. He bought the diamonds from the Van Rooten gal yesterday. Cotter claims she came here to get them back. We thought maybe Cotter had a row with the old man and took them himself. We searched his room. No dice."

Pascal squinted down at the corpse through the smoke from his cigarette. "What was the old man doing with that much in diamonds?"

The leg man shook his head. "The whole thing sounds screwy to me. I can't make head or tail of it. Maybe you better talk to Cotter, Lieutenant."

"Bring him over," Pascal said.

Kelly Cotter didn't have to be brought. He was eager. "Are you, finally, the man in charge?" he asked.

"Could be," Pascal said. "Of course, I have a boss, and he has a boss, the police commissioner, and he has a boss, the mayor, and he has a boss, the—"

"Will you try to make sense!" Cotter exploded.

Nice face, Pascal thought. Good, angry eyes. The well-tailored suit suggested a business executive, but Kelly Cotter's hands were calloused and weathered. They were the hands of a man who used them for work.

"You invited us here?" Pascal said.

"I'm sick of wisecracks," Kelly Cotter said. "I found the girl here. She killed him. I called the cops. And what happens? They suspect *me!* They've torn *my* room to pieces, searched *my* belongings. I tell you, Carla Van Rooten came here shortly before midnight last night. She and the old man drank that bottle of liquor together. She tried to wheedle him out of the diamonds. When he refused, she slugged him with that flower vase."

"The girl says she didn't come at midnight," the leg man said, referring to his book. "She says she came this morning, about five minutes before Cotter found her here. The hotel people bear that out. She has an alibi for the whole evening. She was at home. Pretty well substantiated by her aunt, by servants, by the building personnel where she lives."

"I tell you, she came here last night. I was here when she phoned the old man. I—" Cotter choked on his own sense of futility.

"Take him somewhere and get him to write down the whole story," Pascal said to the leg man, indicating Cotter.

"I don't have to write it down. I can tell you in five minutes," Cotter said.

"I'm kind of slow mentally," Pascal said. "I like to have it all written down—every detail of it. Besides, it'll get you out of my hair. I don't like excitable young men in my hair at the beginning of a case."

"But I tell you, the girl is your murderer! I tell you—"

"Take him away somewhere," Pascal said. "Give him lots of paper and pencils. You just write down the simple facts, Mr. Cotter. When you've done that we'll talk." . . .

In a room down the hall Kelly Cotter sat at a desk. He scowled down at a blank sheet of paper. He was so angry his hands shook. Finally he squared away at the paper and began to write:

STATEMENT OF KELLY COTTER

To Lieutenant Pascal: You asked me to write down the simple facts. Well, they aren't simple! But I'll begin with the most important one:

I did 'not kill George Rawn, which you and your assistants seem to believe. Ironically, I came to New York with him to protect him from danger. Not that I had any notion that there was any risk of violence or murder. I was just afraid someone might try to sell him the Brooklyn Bridge, and in his state of mind he might have been interested in buying it!

I was asleep when the old man was killed. Unfortunately, either my morals are too good or my luck is too bad, because I was sleeping alone and there's nobody to alibi me. I went down the hall to the old man's suite about nine-thirty in the morning and found Carla Van Rooten there and the old man dead. He'd told me, as I was going to bed the night before, that she was coming to see him. He told me not to hang around, because he knew how I felt about Carla Van Rooten, and he said he was entitled to a little fun without my being around to gloom it up.

Naturally, when I found her here with him, I figured she was the one who'd smashed in his head with that silver vase. I called the cops. They decided to make it easy for themselves. They decided *I* was it! They searched my room and ripped my luggage to pieces looking for the diamonds.

For you to understand this at all I'll have to tell you some of the background.

I met George Rawn about six months ago out in Oklahoma. I was working in the oil fields out there. Old George was in his late seventies. He'd done everything in his time, chiefly prospecting for gold. But he'd wound up as a tool wiper in the oil fields. He was a character. I loved to listen to him talk. I used to take him out and buy him a few beers at night, just to listen to him.

Well, one day he told me about a gadget he'd invented for simplifying the capping of oil wells when they came in. It sounded terrific to me. I won't go into the technical details, because you wouldn't understand. I asked him why he hadn't sold it. He said that was because it was only in his head. He'd never made a model of it or drawn a blueprint. Well, I got pretty excited about the idea. I sat up nights with him, making blueprints—I'm a mechanical engineer by trade—and finally a working model.

To cut it short, when the thing was completed we took it to a big oil company. They nearly jumped out of their pants. They offered old George a half-million bucks for the invention, plus a royalty on every one of the gadgets sold.

It was a terrific break for the old man. He floored me by insisting that I share in his good luck, and finally I got myself convinced that I was entitled to 20 per cent. Anyway, one day George and I were broke, and the next day we had more money than either of us ever knew existed.

We did what anyone would, I guess. We bought clothes, and put up at the best hotels, ate food and drank liquor we'd never been able to afford. We threw it around a little. Why not?

One night, after we'd been burning up the town a bit, we wound up in a corner saloon. The old man always insisted on finishing up in a dive of some kind.

"Just so we won't forget we're common people, like everyone else," he'd say.

This night the old man was a little drunk, and when he was drunk he got sentimental. He sat at a corner table with me, turning his drink round and round in his gnarled hand. His pale blue eyes were filled up with tears.

"We've had our fun, Kelly," he said. "Now there are

things I've got to do."

"For instance?" I said.

"I've got to buy diamonds," he said.

"Sure," I said, "sure." I thought he was kidding. "The way you're fixed you can buy out the Aga Khan, if you want."

"Diamonds," he said, "for investment."

"You've got your investment," I said. "The gadget!"

"You didn't know Dolly," he said. "But I promised her, if I ever struck it rich, I'd put some of the money into diamonds—for security, you understand."

"Pardon me," I said, "but I don't understand. What are you talking about—security?"

He looked up at me, and the tears—big ones—ran down his leathery cheeks. "You can always pawn diamonds if you get in a jam," he said.

I knew this was a quote from this Dolly, whoever she was. It came out finally, piece by piece. Dolly O'Connor had been a show girl in a traveling company forty years ago. I guess old George really fell in love with her. I guess she was the only person he could remember loving. He'd wanted to marry her, but he was broke. She knew all there was to know about uncertainty in show business, and she wasn't for jumping from the frying pan into the fire. Maybe she loved old George. He certainly believed she did. But she wasn't for marrying him on expectations. Now, people in show business are always putting any loose change they have into diamonds. It used to be a sort of unwritten law, because, as George had said, you could always pawn them. So apparently Dolly O'Connor told George:

"The day you can show me diamonds worth a thousand dollars that we can hold on to for security—that day, George, I'll marry you."

That day never came. George wrote to her, and the

hope was always just around the corner, but it didn't materialize. Finally, many years after their first meeting, George got word that Dolly had died in a cheap rooming-house in New York. Somehow, he'd raised the money to pay for her funeral.

"Did it up brown," he told me. "But I always swore that I'd buy diamonds if I ever struck it, the way she wanted. So I'm going to New York tomorrow to buy diamonds."

"You don't have to go to New York for that," I said.

His tears seemed to dry up, and a glimmer of excitement crept into his faded eyes. "Ten or twelve years ago I met a fellow in the diamond business," he said. "He was a Dutchman named Van Rooten. He was in the diamond-importing business—rough diamonds, just the way they come out of the mines in South Africa or wherever it is. He said to me, 'Rawn,' he said, 'if you ever do buy those diamonds you're talking about come and see me,' he said. 'You'll get an extra kick out of buying unfinished stones,' he said. 'There's a gamble in it,' he said, 'an exciting gamble. It would appeal to a man like you who's spent his life gambling.'" The old man put his glass down hard on the table. "So I'm going to New York tomorrow to see this Hendrik Van Rooten."

That's how we happened to come here, Lieutenant. I came along for the ride and to keep the old man from being taken too badly. I figured every sharpshooter would be on his trail. You see, the story of the gadget had been in the newspapers, on the radio.

When we got to New York the old man insisted on going to the Bransfield Hotel on lower Fifth Avenue. He'd been in New York nearly thirty years ago, and in those days the Bransfield was the fancy hotel in town. I couldn't convince him that thirty years was thirty years. He got what the management called a "suite," which consisted of those two high-ceilinged rooms with the paper peeling off the walls and Victorian furniture. I took a single room and bath down the hall from him. I guess it's important to mention that there were four other rooms between mine and the old man's bedroom. I couldn't possibly have heard anything that was going on in the "suite" from my room.

As soon as we had lunch that first day we took a cab uptown to the offices of Hendrik Van Rooten, Ltd. They were in a modern office building in the Forties on Fifth Avenue. We went up twenty-two floors in an elevator that had my stomach turned upside down and let ourselves into Van Rooten's office. There was a waiting-room, with leather chairs and a sofa and a thick rug. But there wasn't anyone around.

"Hey!" the old man shouted. "Hey—somebody!"

Nothing happened. Then I noticed that there was a steel door at the far end of the room with a sliding panel in it, and a bell set in the frame alongside it. I rang the bell, and almost instantly the panel slid open and a guy looked out at us.

"Yes?" he said.

"I want to see Mr. Hendrik Van Rooten," the old man said.

"What about?"

"Diamonds," the old man said.

"You can't see him," the face in the panel said.

"Now, look here, son," George Rawn said: "I'm an old friend of Hendrik Van Rooten's. He told me any time I came here he'd see me. Any time, he said."

"He's going to have to break his word," the face said. "He's been dead for two years."

That was a stunner to the old man. "Well, who's in charge here?" he asked.

"Just what is it you want?" the face asked.

"Doggone it, I told you!" the old man bellowed. "I want to buy diamonds!"

"What's your name?"

"Rawn! George Rawn! If you can read, which don't seem likely, maybe you know who I am."

"Just a minute." The panel slid shut.

The old man shook his head. "Dead!" he said. "It don't seem possible. Why, he was a young man! Couldn't have been a day over sixty."

A moment later the steel door opened and we saw what went with the face. He was about five feet two, with hair that stuck out on his head like wet, matted straw.

"This way, Mr. Rawn." From the unctuous way he said it I knew he knew exactly who we were.

After closing and bolting the steel door behind us he led us through an office, filled with filing cabinets and ledgers, to an inner office. He stood aside to let us go in ahead of him. I heard his voice squeak behind us as we went in:

"This is Mr. Rawn, Miss Van Rooten."

There was a flat-topped table in this office, covered with a black baize material. On the table was a delicate-looking set of scales under a glass cover and some pads of shiny white paper. Seated behind the table was a girl. She had gold-colored hair, and a figure that sent little prickles running up and down my back. It was hard to describe her face, because she was wearing dark glasses in harlequin-shaped frames. When you can't see a person's eyes, the whole face becomes sort of blank.

"Thanks, Eddie," the girl said to the little guy. She stood up and held out her hand to the old man. Standing up, the figure was even more so. "I remember my father telling me about you, Mr. Rawn, long ago. I remembered it when I read about your good fortune in the newspapers. I'm Carla Van Rooten." She had a pleasant, low voice, but it was very impersonal.

"I'm glad to know you, Miss Van Rooten," the old man said, "and sorry to hear about your father. This is my partner, Kelly Cotter."

"Mr. Cotter," Carla said, and inclined her head slightly in my direction, almost as though I wasn't there at all.

"Hi," I said.

"I have been running the business since my father's death," Carla said to the old man. "What can I do for you, Mr. Rawn?"

"I want to buy diamonds," he said.

She waved him to a chair beside the table and reseated herself. There was no chair for me, and she just left me standing there. I guess she figured I wasn't important. "I don't know whether you understand, Mr. Rawn, that we are diamond importers. We don't handle finished goods at all."

"Your old man explained that," George said. "He said there was a kind of gamble in buying your kind of stuff. That's why I came here. Gambling is in my blood."

"Eddie, open the safe," Carla said. Then, as an afterthought: "Gentlemen, this is my assistant, Eddie Mostil."

The guy raised his hands over his head like a fighter being introduced from the ring, and went over to a huge safe in the corner. He spun the complicated-looking dials, and finally opened it.

"Bring the stuff on the top shelf," Carla said.

Mostil brought over a tray with half a dozen hunks of stuff on it that looked like dirty ice cubes. He rolled them, like dice out of a cup, onto the black baize table-top.

"Those are diamonds?" the old man asked, after a moment's silence.

"Take one of them over to the window, Mr. Rawn, and loupe it." She handed him a small, double-lensed magnifying glass that you're supposed to fit into your eye. I'd seen watchmakers use them. "Show him how, Eddie."

Mostil took the old man over to the window and showed him how to fit the loupe into his eye.

"That stone," Carla said, in the voice of a lantern-slide lecturer, "has a gletz in it."

"Gletz?" the old man asked.

"It's a fissure, or crack. Do you see it, Mr. Rawn?" He nodded, and she went on: "That's the gamble. When that stone is manufactured, the gletz may run so deep that it cracks the stone in two—maybe part of it splinters. You wouldn't have much left if that happened. On the other hand, maybe the gletz isn't too deep, and you come out with a large, fancy colored stone, worth a fortune."

The old man took the loupe out of his eye and turned to her: "That's why you haven't sold it—on account of that crack?"

"Mr. Rawn, the diamond business is based on what we call illusion," she said. "I have illusion about that stone. I think it will manufacture into high-grade goods. In other words, I don't think it will split or splinter. When someone else comes along who has illusion for it he will pay my price."

"What about the rest of them there on the table?" the old man asked.

Carla picked up one of the murky cubes. "This one is an ingrown," she said. "It has a small stone imbedded in a larger one. Can the cutter get the small stone out without destroying the larger one? Remember, you never get a second chance in this business, Mr. Rawn. Once you start to saw or cleave a stone, the die is cast. You're either right or wrong."

She dropped that stone and picked up another. "This one has a naat in it—that's a sort of knot—an irregularity in the grain. This one has a pique, a speck of foreign matter imbedded in the diamond. They're all speculatives, Mr. Rawn. That's where the gamble lies."

The old man had moved back toward the table and from where he stood he had a clear view of the interior of the safe.

"What's that?" he asked. He pointed to a package, wrapped in brown paper and sealed with heavy wax seals. It was about the size of a large shoe box.

"That's a shipment from the Syndicate," Carla said.

"What syndicate?"

She was really very patient with him. "A diamond trading company of London, England," she said. "They control about ninety-five per cent of the wholesale outlet for rough diamonds in the world, Mr. Rawn. In our business you have to be on the Syndicate List. Periodically we are sent a consignment of goods. We know how many carats, and the type of stones involved, but we don't see the shipment in advance and we take whatever comes." She smiled faintly. "We just paid a hundred thousand dollars for the contents of that box."

The old man's eyes widened. "But you haven't opened it?"

"I'm not going to," Carla said. "I've already arranged to sell it, in the dark, for a ten per cent profit."

"You mean somebody's going to buy it without looking at it?"

"In the dark, we call it," she said.

"Holy smoke!" old George said.

"My buyer may make a big profit," she said. "He

may not. With the market what it is, I'm satisfied with ten per cent. If I opened the package, my buyer would no longer have illusion. He'd know exactly what he was getting. This way, we're both taking a chance; I, that I'm passing up a much larger profit; he, that he's stuck with a loss."

"That *is* gambling!" old George said.

"Yes, Mr. Rawn, that is gambling," Carla said.

Old George drew a deep breath. "I'll offer you a fifteen per cent profit," he said.

There was a squeaking sound from Eddie Mostil in the background.

"Look, George; take it easy!" I said. "A hundred and fifteen thousand dollars is a lot of money, even for you!"

Not a muscle of Carla Van Rooten's face moved. I couldn't see her eyes because of those blasted glasses. "I'm already committed to my friend," she said.

"How much could your friend expect to make after offering you ten per cent?" old George asked.

"Ten for himself, if he was lucky," Carla said.

"I'll give you a hundred and twenty-one thousand," the old man said promptly. "That covers you *and* your friend."

Carla reached out and her fingers played with the rough cubes on the table. Then she looked straight through me at Eddie Mostil. "Get Stanley Wyman on the phone, Eddie," she said.

"I can't," Eddie wailed. "He's flying east from Chicago today. There's no way to reach him."

"Look; forget the whole thing, Miss Van Rooten," I said. "George is crazy to go for a deal like this."

"Shut up, Kelly," George said. "It's my money. If I want to have fun with it I will." He took a checkbook out of his pocket. "I've had funds transferred to me here in New York, Miss Van Rooten. I'll write you a check for $121,000 right now. You can send your assistant to get it certified."

For the first time I sensed that she was really excited. Why not? The whole store was probably sucker bait, and the sucker was biting.

"At least, let someone else tell you how crazy you are," I said to George, "someone who knows diamonds."

"I told you to shut up, Kelly," he said. "Well, Miss Van Rooten?"

"Stanley would probably jump at it if he was here," she said, more to herself than anyone else.

"You can't do it, Carla," Eddie Mostil said. "You promised Stanley."

"Can you wait till Mr. Wyman gets back to New York, Mr. Rawn?"

Old George grinned at her. "Nope," he said. "I got illusion about that package of stuff. Right now I'm ready to gamble on it. Tomorrow I might not. How about you, Miss Van Rooten? Aren't you in a gambling mood?"

The dark, harlequin glasses were fixed on him in a long stare. The buzzer in the outer office sounded, but no one paid it any attention. "It's a deal, Mr. Rawn," she said.

"No!" Eddie Mostil wailed. "You promised Stanley!"

"Get Mr. Rawn the package from the safe, Eddie," she said.

The old man wrote a check in his spidery handwriting. "We'll wait here till you have it certified, Miss Van Rooten."

"That won't be necessary," she said.

Eddie brought the package from the safe. He didn't seem to want to let go of it, and the old man snatched it away from him. He turned it over and over, staring at the heavy, customhouse seals. "In the dark!" he muttered. "I like that! That's gambling!"

I should have stayed in bed, I told myself. I'd come all the way to New York to keep him from being taken, and it had happened right in front of my eyes.

"You're to be congratulated on your footwork," I said to Carla.

"Shut up, Kelly," the old man said. He looked up at Carla. "Any more red tape?" he asked.

"None," she said. "Unless you'd like me to send for a man from the Protective Agency to guard you on your way home." The dark glasses turned just a fraction my way, and I could imagine that the eyes behind them were laughing at me.

"Don't ride Kelly," the old man said, grinning. "He hasn't got gambling in his blood like you and me, Miss Van Rooten. But he's a real good man in a fight. The best."

"When the opposition is male!" I said sourly.

The old man tucked the box under his arm—121,000 bucks' worth of illusion—and we started out of the office. Carla came with us. The least she could do was go to the door with us.

When we got through the steel door into the outside reception-room there was somebody there. I remembered having heard the buzzer while Carla was putting over her deal with the old man, the buzzer nobody had noticed.

The person in the reception-room was a man, about six feet six inches tall, wearing a suit that fitted him like an outsize circus tent. It hung on him in folds and drapes; it fluttered around his bony frame as a draft blew through the open steel door. He was completely bald, and if there had been a fringe of hair left around his head it had been shaved tight to his skull with a razor. He wore large, steel-rimmed glasses, and the lenses were so thick that they magnified his eyes grotesquely. The pupils looked as large as coal-black dimes.

"Miss Van Rooten?" His voice was husky; like a fighter who has been hit too often and too hard in the Adam's apple.

"Yes," Carla said. "If you'll wait just a moment—"

The thick-lensed glasses focused on the package George Rawn had tucked under his arm. If anything, the eyes behind them grew wider and larger. "That—that package!" he whispered. "Is that your shipment from the Syndicate?"

"I'm afraid that's none of your business, my friend," Carla said.

"Just a minute. Please!" He moved over to the door to block our exit. "My name is Jan Spivak." He pronounced Jan as though it was spelled with a "Y." "I am a broker, Miss Van Rooten, representing a client who shall remain nameless. I have come to make an offer on that shipment."

"I have already sold it," Carla said.

"No!" Mr. Spivak moaned. "That is impossible."

"I have just sold it to Mr. Rawn," Carla said, indicating the old man.

Spivak shook his shiny bald head from side to side as if he were suffering intolerable pain. "Sir, you have made this purchase for speculative purposes, I trust. I see, from the seals being intact, that you have made this purchase in the dark."

Old George winked at me, as much as to say, "See? I'm not such a bad gambler, at that."

"May I inquire, sir," Spivak asked, "what price you paid?"

"Now, if I was to tell you that," old George said, "you might think I wasn't a smart operator."

"I would not question your intelligence, sir. It is already proved by this purchase," Spivak said. He ran his tongue slowly over his upper and lower lips. "My client, who shall remain nameless," he said, "is prepared to make it possible for you to realize a handsome profit, sir."

"Now, that's real nice of your client," old George said. He was the cat that had just swallowed two lovebirds!

"Name your price, sir," Spivak said.

"Now, I don't happen to have a price," old George said. "What are you offering, Mr.—?"

"Spivak, sir. Jan Spivak. I—I, sir—cannot very well make an offer without knowing what you have paid."

"That's your problem, Mr. Spivak," old George said.

Spivak writhed. "One hundred and fifteen thousand dollars," he said.

"You think we ought to take a taxi downtown?" old George asked me.

"Talk to the man, George," I said. I was getting interested. Maybe George was going to get off the hook, at that.

"One hundred and twenty thousand," Spivak said.

"Kind of warm for this time of year, ain't it?" old George said.

Spivak swallowed hard. "One hundred twenty-five," he whispered.

"It's been a great privilege meeting you, Miss Van Rooten," old George said. "I reckon we've taken up too much of your time already. Come on, Kelly."

"One hundred thirty!" Spivak said, the whisper tortured.

I saw Carla and Eddie Mostil exchange glances. Eddie looked as though his best friend had just stabbed him to the heart. If Spivak had come half an hour sooner they'd have been in clover.

"One thirty-five!" Spivak said. He reached out to the doorjamb to support himself. He was collapsing inside his suit.

"Sorry, Mr. Spivak," old George said, "but I reckon I'm not interested."

"Please!" Spivak moaned. He held both his hands, palms out, as if to keep old George back from the door. "I can see you are not a man to be trifled with. I will make you my top offer." His eyes seemed to bulge and pulsate behind the thick lenses. "One hundred and fifty thousand!" he whispered dramatically.

There was a squeak of pain from Eddie Mostil, who was standing behind me. I saw Carla Van Rooten lift her hand slowly to her cheek. It was a gesture of downright disbelief.

"In case you should happen to think, sir, that this is just talk," Spivak said, "I will show you." He unbuttoned his coat and reached inside its folds. He looked like a man wrestling with himself. Presently he produced a huge leather wallet, said wallet being attached to his midsection by a fine steel chain. His fingers fumbled the wallet open and he extracted from it more cash than I have ever seen in my life. He began to count off thousand-dollar bills.

"Now, just a minute, Mr. Spivak," old George interrupted, before Spivak had counted more than fifteen. Spivak stopped counting, one crisp, green thousand-dollar bill fluttering in his fingers. "I'm not saying no and I'm not saying yes," old George said. "I just made this purchase, you understand."

"Never, sir, was anyone offered such a quick profit," Spivak said.

"It's too quick," old George said.

"Now, look, George—" I said.

"Take it easy, Kelly. Take it easy. When a man buys something for no other reason than to pleasure himself, he likes to savor it for a while. A fellow who likes to eat don't gobble up his food, Mr. Spivak, and a fellow who is pleasuring himself don't like to gobble up the pleasure. He likes to savor it a while."

"George, you'll never get another offer like this," I said.

"Shut up, Kelly," he said cheerfully. "Now, here's how it is, Mr. Spivak: After I've done a bit of savoring maybe I'd be interested in listening to you again. Maybe not. But you could try me."

"When, sir?" Spivak whispered.

"Hard to say, Mr. Spivak. But I'm lodging at the Bransfield Hotel. You could try phoning me there. When I'm through savoring, maybe we could talk business." The old man turned to Carla with a happy smile. "I've really enjoyed myself, Miss Van Rooten. I'm indebted to you," he said. "Come on, Kelly."

We walked out of there, old George carrying the sealed box, and leaving three people behind us in varying degrees of disbelief and collapse.

I guess you don't need much imagination to know that old George was very pleased with himself. He chuckled over Spivak's discomfiture all the way downtown in the taxi. I admit I felt better. Spivak obviously wanted that shipment so badly he'd certainly be back. After George had enjoyed himself enough he'd probably sell him the box.

"Are you going to open it?" I asked George.

"Can't make up my mind," he said. "Say, this diamond business is a crazy business, Kelly. Stuff seems to be worth more when you don't know what you're buying than when you do!"

"I hope the hotel has got a good burglar-proof safe," I said.

"You don't figure I'd hand this over to some nincompoop of a hotel clerk!" George said. "I'm hanging on to this myself."

"George, for heaven's sake—"

"Kelly, you've been a danged blasted nuisance all day!" he said. "Leave me be, son. Leave me have my fun."

I don't know what George did with that package when we got back to the hotel. He went to his suite alone, acting very coy about not wanting me to come with him. He was alone there for a couple of hours or more. I guess he took a nap, because when he called my room he bawled me out for letting so much time go by. He wanted to go out to dinner.

When I joined him I asked him about the diamonds.

He looked wise. "Nobody's going to find 'em, Kelly. Not even the rats in this old joint."

So we went to dinner and ate and drank too much. It was about eleven-thirty when we got back to the hotel. George suggested we have a nightcap in his rooms. He dug a bottle out of his bureau and got us some glasses from the bathroom. He'd just poured out a couple of hookers when the phone rang. As nearly as I can remember this is exactly what he said:

"Hello...Yes, this is George Rawn...Oh, hello! Sure—sure...No—no, I'm still savoring." And he chuckled. "Of course. When?...Tonight? Well, why not? Be a great pleasure...Sure; I'll be here." And he hung up the phone. "The Van Rooten girl wants to see me," he said. "Now. She'll be here in ten minutes."

"I'll bet she wants to see you," I said. "You did her out of about thirty thousand dollars' profit. I can even tell you what she's going to say to you. She's going to tell you that there was some mistake about the value of the shipment. She's going to appeal to your sense of fair play to let her have the box back. She may offer you a small profit as a token of good will. Then *she'll* deal with brother Spivak and make the killing."

The old man shook his head. "Kelly, I don't know how you've got along so good in life, always suspecting people. Now, I tell you what. You run along to your room and get some sleep."

"I'm staying right here," I said. "I'm not going to stand by and let that dame give you the works."

"You're going to your room—or any place you like, so long as it ain't here," George said. "I'm having fun, Kelly, and you insist on glooming it up. The way you act you'd think I was in my second childhood, or something. I still know the time of day, Kelly. Now, you skedaddle."

I knew there wasn't any use arguing with him. "Okay," I said. "I'll be in my room in case you need me."

He laughed and patted me on the shoulder. "It'll be a sad day when I don't know how to handle a pretty girl, Kelly. A sad day!"

That was the last thing he ever said to me, Lieutenant—the last time I ever saw him alive. I went to my room. I lay on the bed, smoking and reading. I figured maybe he'd call me when Carla left, but when it got to be about three o'clock I couldn't keep my eyes open any longer. I turned off the light and went to sleep...

It was nearly nine o'clock when I woke up. I called George's room, and got no answer. I figured he'd gone downstairs for breakfast and was still there. I shaved and got dressed as quickly as I could, and then I started down the hall to the elevator. I told you there were four rooms between mine and George's. When I came abreast of George's room I saw the door was open. I went in, really expecting to find the chambermaid there.

When I went through the door I found George lying on the floor. There was a nasty wound on the side of his head, and his thin white hair was matted with blood. On the carpet beside his body was a silver flower vase I remembered seeing on the mantelpiece the night before. The room had been torn to pieces by a thorough search.

I heard someone give a little gasp, and I spun around. There was Carla Van Rooten, backed up against the wall, her hands pressed hard against her mouth, staring down at George through those black harlequin glasses.

On the table in the center of the room were the two bathroom tumblers and what was left of the bottle of whisky—maybe three drinks out of the quart we'd opened the night before.

Lieutenant, I loved that old guy. I knew he was dead from the way he lay there. I didn't have to try his pulse to find out. I could feel anger surging up in me so violently that I began to shake all over. I had a pretty clear picture of what had happened—I thought. This girl had sat there with him all night, drinking with him, arguing with him to let her have the diamonds back, and finally, when everything else failed, slugging him with that flower vase and then searching the place. He was a pretty old guy and pretty unsteady when he'd been drinking. He would have been a pushover for a wiry young girl.

I didn't say anything to Carla. I shut the door, locked it, and put the key in my pocket. Then I called the switchboard downstairs and told them there'd been a murder, to call the cops, and that I had the murderer there in the room.

I hung up the phone and turned to Carla. "A nice night's work," I said bitterly.

"You—you think *I* killed him?" She sounded as though I'd slapped her. "But I just got here, Mr. Cotter—a matter of seconds before you did."

"My, how time flies!" I said. "From midnight to nine-thirty in the morning seems like a matter of seconds!"

There's no use going on with that dialogue, Lieutenant. A lot of people came soon—the house dick, the prowl-car cops, the man from the D.A.'s office, and finally your staff. They asked a lot of questions, and instead of taking hold of the obvious, they decided *I* was their meat! So the Van Rooten girl has an alibi! Well, I tell you it can be broken if you'll try! It's so obvious! Why should I kill old George for the diamonds—which they can't find! I don't have to steal or murder to get by. Besides, old George was my closest and best friend.

That's my statement, Lieutenant. It's the truth and nothing but the truth.

(Signed) KELLY COTTER...

The living-room of the two-room suite at the Bransfield which had been occupied by old George Rawn had that special look which hotel rooms have when they've been made ready for new occupants—dusted, characterlessly neat, painfully in order. Lieutenant Pascal of Homicide let himself in with the passkey he'd gotten at the desk. He looked around, and then sat down in an uncomfortable armchair near the window. He took a folded document from his pocket and opened it. It consisted of several sheets of thin legal tissue, covered with single-spaced typing. It was a carbon copy of Kelly Cotter's statement.

He read it slowly, as if he hoped to find something

hidden between the lines. Finally he sighed, folded it up again, and stuffed it in his pocket. The ash fell off his cigarette and dribbled down the front of his blue suit. He ignored it. Presently there was a knock at the door.

"Come in," Pascal said.

Carla Van Rooten came into the room. She was wearing a tailored dark-gray gabardine suit with a white ruffled shirtwaist showing at her neck. She was hatless, and the golden, shoulder-length hair glittered in the sunlight from the windows. The tinted harlequin glasses were missing, and Pascal, who had been bothered by them on their first meeting, thought he understood why she wore them. Her eyes were wide, blue, childlike, and a little frightened. Something of the coolly competent picture she had presented on their first meeting was missing. Somehow, with her eyes unmasked, she seemed very feminine and in need of protection.

"They told me downstairs to come straight up," she said. She glanced around the room as if she was afraid she might see some sign of yesterday's violence still there.

"It's all cleaned up," Pascal said. "Sit down, Miss Van Rooten, and thanks for coming."

She sat down on the frayed lounge facing Pascal's chair. "What has happened to Kelly Cotter?" she asked.

"I have his statement here," Pascal said, tapping his pocket. "We held him overnight, but he's being released. I really didn't have anything on him, Miss Van Rooten. But an arrest looks good, you understand. We have to look good in this business."

"I don't believe you mean that," Carla said.

Pascal grinned. "Maybe not. But the young man is a little impetuous. He was making charges against you, ignoring the evidence. He needed what we call a cooling-off period. It's a popular procedure these days, even if it doesn't make any sense."

"I take it from you that you—you've written me off," Carla said.

"Not at all," Pascal said cheerfully. "I just know you didn't kill George Rawn five minutes before Cotter found you here. I also know you weren't here earlier in the evening. Until I can think up some other way to make you fit the part of a murderer you're free as air."

He laughed outright as he saw the fear creep into her eyes. "I have a very low-grade sense of humor," he said. Then his forehead contracted in a frown. "But there's an awful lot I don't understand about this, Miss Van Rooten. For instance, I find it hard to believe that a man would buy a hundred and twenty-one thousand dollars' worth of something he never saw."

"It was odd for someone like George Rawn, who knew nothing about diamonds," Carla said. "But buying in the dark is standard practice in my business. It happens every day."

"But the stuff in that package—which I wish we could find—might be worthless!" Pascal said.

"Oh, no," Carla said. "The Syndicate makes allotments to the people on its list. We know exactly how many rough stones were in that package, and their weight in carats. The one hundred thousand dollars I paid for them is a fair wholesale price. The gamble lies in what the stones will be worth after they're manufactured."

"Let's go over this once more," Pascal said. "Why *did* you come to see George Rawn yesterday morning?"

Carla looked down at her lacquered finger tips for a moment. "I have a—a friend," she said. "A man named Stanley Wyman. He used to be an importer. He was on the Syndicate List, just as my firm is. But he got into some kind of trouble with the Syndicate and they took him off the list. That means he no longer had access to diamonds on the wholesale market."

"What kind of trouble did Mr. Wyman have with the Syndicate?"

"I don't know, exactly," Carla said. "Stanley is a rather excitable, hotheaded man. He probably made a complaint about a shipment; he may even have accused the Syndicate of putting something over on him. They dropped him."

"And that left him out of business," Pascal said.

Carla nodded.

"Broke?" Pascal asked.

"He had a great deal of money tied up in the trade abroad," she said. "Unless he could do business on this side he was in a tough spot. You can't bring money out of England, you know. Unless he could do business with English firms over here, those assets abroad were frozen. He would only be broke in the sense that he couldn't get at his money."

"Let's get back to your visit to George Rawn," Pascal said. "High finance is a little out of my line."

"The Syndicate had a sight about a month ago," Carla said. "That means that we on the list put in our bids for a certain amount of goods. I agreed to take a hundred thousand dollars' worth. You understand, Lieutenant, you have to buy regularly or you're dropped from the list."

"Sounds like a good, solid monopoly," Pascal said.

"It's always been that way, Lieutenant. Well, Stanley came to me and asked me if I was buying at this sight. I told him I was. He said he'd give me a ten per cent profit, in the dark. He wanted to remain active in the business. He's been trying for months to get back in the good graces of the Syndicate." Carla raised her delicate shoulders. "The diamond market isn't too good at the moment. I have a good deal of stuff on hand. A ten per cent profit seemed like good business to me, so I agreed to let Stanley have the shipment."

"But—?"

"Mr. Rawn came along," she said. "He offered to pay a price which would give me my ten per cent and also give Stanley ten per cent on what he would have paid. I couldn't reach Stanley. He was flying east from Chicago. I had to make the decision myself. Knowing the market, I thought Stanley would be tickled to death to take his ten per cent profit. So I sold the shipment to Mr. Rawn."

"But Wyman wasn't pleased?" Pascal said.

Carla made a wry face. "He blew his top," she said. "He said he had already made a deal with a manufacturer in Chicago for the stuff at much more than the ten per cent I'd made for him. He accused me of breaking my word to him. He—well, he was furious about the whole transaction. I felt bad about it, because I know he's had a rough time since the Syndicate dropped him. I decided to come to see Mr. Rawn, put my cards on the table, and ask him to sell the shipment back to me. I was prepared to offer him a small profit if he would do it."

Pascal smiled. He was remembering Kelly Cotter's statement. Kelly had predicted this was exactly what Carla wanted of old George, although he'd given it another motivation.

'You're sure you didn't want the goods back in order to make a deal with Jan Spivak?" Pascal asked.

"Certainly not," Carla said indignantly.

"That was Cotter's idea," Pascal said.

"Mr. Cotter has had a lot of fancy ideas about me," Carla said.

"Just who is Spivak?"

"I haven't the faintest idea," Carla said. "He said he was a broker. I thought I knew all the brokers in New York but I'd never seen him before."

"Why would he offer such a high price for the shipment?" Pascal asked.

"I'm not a mind reader, Lieutenant. There are a lot of screwballs in the diamond business. I've told you, it's based largely on illusion. Maybe Spivak—"

"Had an overdose of illusion?"

"Could be," Carla said.

"If we recover the stones we may find out the answer," Pascal said. "Spivak may have known something."

"He couldn't know anything," Carla said. "Let me explain the mechanics to you: I tell the Syndicate I'll buy a hundred thousand dollars' worth of goods, specifying the type—crinkles, shapes, maccles, blocks, flats. Those are trade classifications for rough diamonds, Lieutenant. The Syndicate makes a package for me, listing the number of stones and their weight in carats. It's shipped to this country. We don't have to pay a customs duty, since they're not manufactured. But on this end the customs people check the shipment—they weigh the goods to see that the carat weight is as declared on the invoice. Then they seal the box, just as it was when Mr. Rawn bought it. That box has to contain exactly what the Syndicate specified. Spivak couldn't know anything, because there isn't anything to know."

"Nobody could have been shipping you the crown jewels?" Pascal suggested. "Without your knowing it?"

"They had to be rough diamonds, weighing a specified amount, or the customs wouldn't pass them," Carla said.

"Well, that's that," Pascal said.

Carla looked straight at the Lieutenant. "There's one thing, Mr. Pascal."

"Yes?"

"If that box has been opened we'll never be able to identify the goods. Manufactured stones can be identified, but diamonds in the rough—" She let it go with a shrug.

"You mean they can be sold on the market and there's no way of our knowing that they are the goods you sold George Rawn?"

"No way at all," Carla said. "We could suspect, if someone was silly enough to try marketing them in a lump, but we could never prove."

"Then here's hoping my hunch is right," Pascal said.

"What is your hunch, Lieutenant?"

"The old man told Cotter he'd hidden the stones somewhere. He said not even the rats in this hotel could find them. I'm hoping he was right and that I may turn out to be smarter than a rat—before someone else!"

"But where could he hide them? You've searched these rooms."

"Including the cracks in the ceiling!" Pascal said. "Look, Miss Van Rooten; the old man was killed for those stones. I'm still playing a hunch that the murderer didn't get them. I have to play that hunch, or throw in the towel. Unless the murderer has to keep looking, and we can catch him at it, he's gotten away clean, as far as I can see."

"You give up easier than I do," said a voice from the doorway.

Pascal jerked his head around. Kelly Cotter stood there, a truculent expression on his face.

"Well, well, Mr. Cotter!" Pascal said. "I see you made it."

"And I can think of better things to do than sit around theorizing," Kelly said.

Twenty-four hours of mounting rage, fanned by twelve of them in the city jail, where he'd been taken after writing his statement and held as a material witness, had left Kelly Cotter seething.

He gave Carla a curt little nod. "I see you've still got the police in your pocket," he said.

"If you think for one minute," Carla blazed, "that I—"

"I've been thinking for twenty-four hours!" Kelly said. "The old man is dead because of that fancy deal with you. I don't know whose side you're on—Spivak's or your friend Wyman's or just your own—but I do know you're in it—but deep!"

"Please," Pascal said wearily. "Stage your bout in private. Tell me, Cotter, where did the old man hide the diamonds?"

"Do you think if I knew I'd have stood around while your men tore my suits and luggage and room to pieces?" Kelly said.

"I do, if you happen to have them hidden somewhere yourself," Pascal said.

"Look," Kelly said; "old George was my friend. I didn't want his diamonds. What would I do with diamonds? The whole deal was a gag—the old man was hipped on the subject."

"I know," Pascal said. "The late, lamented Dolly O'Connor."

"Well, we stepped into a hornet's nest without knowing it," Kelly said. "And unless I'm very much mistaken Miss Van Rooten, here, is the queen bee."

"Different species of bee," Pascal said. "Where could the old man have hidden those stones, Cotter? According to your statement he *did* hide them."

"He didn't tell me," Kelly said. "Maybe he told Miss Van Rooten when she came to see him that night."

"She didn't come that night," Pascal said patiently. "She didn't come till the next morning, a few minutes before you got here."

"She talked to him on the phone. She made an appointment to see him shortly before midnight," Kelly said.

"That's not true!" Carla said angrily. "I never called him. I never saw him or talked to him after you both left my office with the diamonds."

"You just walked up here unannounced yesterday morning?" Pascal asked mildly.

"That's right!" Carla said. "I asked at the desk if he was in, and they said he was. Frankly, I didn't want him to prepare for me. I—"

"Go on!" Kelly said.

"I wanted him unprepared," Carla said defiantly. "I thought I might have a better chance of persuading him if he had no time at all to think. That's perfectly sound business tactics!"

"What did you talk about the night before—when you came here after your phone call?" Kelly demanded.

"I didn't phone him! I didn't come here!" Carla said. Her voice was shrill with anger.

"That's great," Kelly said. "When I heard the conversation! When I heard him make the date with you!"

"Now, just a minute," Pascal said, in his quiet way. "I read your statement very carefully, Mr. Cotter. I don't remember your saying you heard Miss Van Rooten's voice on the phone, or that George Rawn actually said it had been Miss Van Rooten on the phone." He took the statement out of his pocket and fumbled through the papers. "Here it is. Quote: 'As nearly as I can remember, this is exactly what he said: "Hello... Yes, this is George Rawn... Oh, hello! Sure—sure... No—no. I'm still savoring... Of course. When?... Tonight? Well, why not? Be a great pleasure... Sure; I'll be here." He hung up the phone. "The Van Rooten girl wants to see me. Now. She'll be here in ten minutes."' Close quote."

"Well?" Kelly said.

"That's your statement," Pascal said. "According to that, he didn't say it was Miss Van Rooten on the phone. According to that, somebody else could have been making the appointment for Miss Van Rooten."

"So what?" Kelly said.

"So someone figured that the old man would receive Miss Van Rooten when he wouldn't somebody else. Could be, you know. Someone calls and says, 'I'm Joe Doaks, calling for Carla Van Rooten. Will you see her if she comes over to your hotel now?'"

"Are you telling me that's what happened?" Kelly asked.

"It could have," Pascal said, squinting up at Kelly through cigarette smoke.

"If Mr. Cotter's statement is true, it *did* happen that way," Carla said. "Because I never phoned."

Kelly was silent for a moment. He felt a little uncomfortable about his persistent attack on Carla. After all, she did have an alibi. Then he snapped his fingers. "Spivak!" he said. "George referred in that phone call to the speech he made in the office about 'savoring his pleasure.' It was Spivak he was talking to."

"It might have been," Pascal said.

"Spivak's your murderer," Kelly said.

"My, my," said Pascal, grinning. "How your convictions do jump around, Mr. Cotter!" . . .

Despite his anger, his suspicions, and his urgent desire to see George Rawn's murderer made to pay for his crime, Kelly Cotter was a normal young man, and a normal young man could not be in Carla Van Rooten's presence too long without being aware of her femaleness, tailored suit and businesslike attitude notwithstanding.

When Pascal seemed through with the interview Kelly went out in the hall with the young lady. Pascal said he wanted to think—"not that I'm very hopeful of the outcome."

"I guess I've been a little quick on the trigger from the beginning," Kelly said. He was trying to decide whether to go down the hall to his room or to the elevator with Carla.

"You have," Carla said.

"You understand—what seems commonplace to you in your business," Kelly said, "sounded pretty whacky to me."

"I suppose so," Carla said.

"I do owe you an apology, I guess," Kelly said. "I—well, I guess I haven't exactly endeared myself to you, accusing you of—well, pretty much everything."

Carla smiled at him for the first time. "I've been wondering if anyone who made so many wild charges in the space of five minutes was equipped to take care of himself."

Kelly flushed. "People have a way of looking bad in a strange setting," he said. "Maybe you'd let me buy you a cup of coffee, or something—just to show there's no hard feeling."

"I'd love it," Carla said. "To tell you the truth, Lieutenant Pascal got me down here before I'd had any breakfast."

Kelly felt better as they walked to the elevator together. He felt New York wasn't quite so big, or friendless, or violent as he had thought it was for the last twelve hours. "There's a dining-room here in the hotel," he said. "Or would you like to go somewhere else?"

"It'll be fine here," Carla said.

As they stepped out of the elevator into the lobby

Kelly slid his fingers under Carla's arm. "This way," he said.

They hadn't taken two steps, however, before their way was blocked by someone new to Kelly. A man bore down on them, dark, eager, with wide, excited black eyes.

"Carla!" he shouted, for the whole lobby to hear, seized Carla's shoulders with hairy-backed hands, and planted a kiss as near to her mouth as he could get as she turned her head quickly to one side. "Carla, I've been out of my *mind* with worry. Are you all right? They haven't mistreated you?"

"Please, Stanley!" Carla said, disengaging herself from the grip on her shoulders. "Of course I'm all right. This is Mr. Cotter, Stanley. Mr. Wyman—Mr. Cotter."

"Oh!" Stanley Wyman said. He took a handkerchief out of the breast pocket of his suit and mopped his forehead with it. "I've been waiting for you to come down, Carla."

He paid no more attention to Kelly, who stood there with the hackles rising on the back of his neck.

"I've got to talk to you at once," Wyman said. "Where can we go?" He used his hands expressively when he spoke, and Kelly noticed he wore a huge diamond in a platinum setting on the little finger of his right hand.

"Mr. Cotter has just invited me to have some breakfast with him," Carla said.

"Splendid," Wyman said. "Splendid. Of course, I want to talk to him, too. This whole thing is a disaster."

Kelly knew he meant the loss of the diamonds, not George Rawn's murder. "There's a dining-room down that flight of stairs," he said.

"I know," Wyman said.

He took Carla's arm possessively and led her away,

leaving Kelly to bring up the rear. He summoned the headwaiter. He demanded a corner booth. He gave loud orders that they were not to be disturbed by anyone. He maneuvered it so that he and Carla sat on one side of the booth, with Kelly facing them across the table. He made it flamboyantly clear that he was holding Carla's hand.

"It's been too dreadful for you, my sweet," Wyman said. "But what news? Have the police located the shipment?"

"They haven't found the shipment, Stanley," Carla said.

"But that's insane!" Wyman said. "Where could that old goat have hidden them?"

"That old goat," Kelly said in a dangerously quiet voice, "happens to have been my best friend, Mr. Wyman. I happen to be concerned with catching his murderer."

"My dear boy," Wyman said. "My condolences, and all that sort of thing. But I'm in a mess. Carla had promised that shipment and I made a deal for it. Those goods must be found."

"Aren't you overlooking the fact," Kelly said, "that, even when they are found, they belong to George Rawn and are now a part of his estate?"

"The man has heirs!" Wyman said. "The goods can be bought from them. By the way, who are his heirs?"

"I haven't any idea," Kelly said. "He had no family. I don't know if he'd ever made a will."

Wyman snorted. "The whole thing is preposterous. Personally, I don't believe for one minute the old man could hide those stones. The murderer got them." He turned his black eyes full on Kelly, "Don't you think so, Mr. Cotter?"

"It's possible," Kelly said. "Look, Carla; you wanted breakfast. Have you decided what you'd like?"

"Breakfast can wait!" Wyman shouted. "I've only got a few minutes. Now, Carla, you've explained that it was all a mistake? That you were committed to sell the shipment to me? That may stand up in court, you know."

"I've explained everything, Stanley," Carla said.

"Good, good. I'm going to file an official claim to the shipment now. You must keep me posted. You'll be on the inside with the police, of course, and you'll know what's happening."

"I have a hunch the police will be interested in you, too, Wyman," Kelly said.

"In me? What for?" Wyman said.

"Because of the way you drool when those diamonds are mentioned," Kelly said. "Somebody wanted them badly enough to kill for them. They may get the idea you had a strong motive, Wyman."

"Nonsense!" Wyman said. "Carla, I hate to leave you, but I must. I've got to try to pacify my clients. I'll be in touch every chance I get."

Backed into the corner of the booth, Carla had little sparring room in which to ward off Wyman's kiss on her cheek. He stood up, nodded abruptly at Kelly, and galloped away across the room.

"Stanley is odd," she murmured. "You have to get to know him."

Kelly opened his mouth to reply, and then changed his mind. He beckoned to the waiter. "Orange juice?" he asked Carla.

They ordered breakfast. When the waiter had gone, Kelly said, "I take it Wyman is an old family friend."

"We—Stanley and I—have been sort of unofficially engaged for some time," Carla said. A faint pink rose in her cheeks as she said it.

"You're kidding," Kelly said.

"You object, Mr. Cotter?"

"Oh, he's in love with you, all right," Kelly said, "particularly when he looks at that dollar sign in the middle of your forehead. Marry you, and he has the financial backing of Hendrik Van Rooten, Ltd., he's back on the Syndicate List, and he's in business again. Oh, he loves you, all right."

"Now, look, Mr. Cotter," Carla said; "we were just getting on a footing where we didn't shriek at each other. My private life is my own affair. Please leave it that way."

"Anything you say," Kelly said. He took a deep breath. "Have you read any good books lately, Miss Van Rooten?"

From there on, the breakfast was a little stiff and formal, until Kelly got talking about old George Rawn. Carla hadn't heard his story. It was safe ground, because Kelly had no reason to hide what he had felt for the old man nor his eagerness to see the murderer caught. He liked the way Carla reacted to the story. She had a capacity for warm feeling that she tried very hard to hide on other occasions.

She, in turn, told him something about herself: her childhood with a father who had become a widower when she was two; of travels all over the world, never staying put in one place long enough to make friends; of having the diamond business instilled in her from the moment of her earliest recollection.

It was a strange business, with strange ethics. You took a man's word about whether anyone had seen the goods before you; you took his own word on one or two other points, but from there in you were on your own in a pack of wolves. You could meet them at the Diamond Club, where they glared, kibitzed, and insulted one another as they bought and sold. And after you made a deal and shook hands on it, you counted your fingers to make sure they were all there. It was a business full of angles, and around the corner of each angle lay a stropping—a rooking, a disaster.

"A tough business for a woman," Kelly said.

"It leaves its mark on you," Carla said. "It has a tendency to make you everlastingly suspicious of people. It—"

"Except when they plant a big, wet kiss on your cheek," Kelly said. "Then you know it's love."

"We were getting along so nicely," Carla said. She pushed away from the table and stood up. "I've got to get back to the office. Things will have piled up. I can't leave it all to Eddie Mostil."

"I'm sorry you have to go," Kelly said. "Will I see you again?"

"I don't imagine Lieutenant Pascal is through with us," she said.

"Does he have to make my dates for me? Or do I have to ask Stanley's permission?"

"Good-by, Mr. Cotter," she said. . . .

Left alone, Kelly began thinking about his own problems. So far as he knew, it was going to be up to him to arrange for George Rawn's funeral and to make the attempt to locate any family or relatives, even though old George had often said he was quite alone. There were people out in Oklahoma who knew George and might have information; the oil company to whom they had sold the gadget should be notified. There was also a lawyer in Oklahoma City who was handling their affairs.

Kelly went to the desk, picked up a dozen telegraph blanks and took the elevator upstairs, deciding to write the messages in his room. He hesitated outside the door of old George's suite, but he heard Pascal's placid voice in conversation with someone. He went on down the hall to his own room, put the key in the lock, and opened the door.

He was confronted by wreckage. His clothes, which he had put back in the closet and the bureau drawers, were scattered about the place. The bed had been ripped to pieces. His luggage was once more in the center of the floor, opened, searched. And, standing with his back to the bureau, gripping the edges of it to support his sagging legs, was Stanley Wyman, his face the color of chalk.

Kelly shut the door and stood with his back against it. "Well, well," he said. "And to what do I owe the pleasure, et cetera, et cetera?"

"It's simple enough," Wyman said. "I thought perhaps *after* the police had searched here you'd consider this the safest place to hide the shipment. They wouldn't be likely to search again, now would they? You must understand, my whole business career depends on recovering that shipment."

"Which doesn't belong to you."

"A technicality," Wyman said. "I'll buy from the rightful owner or owners."

"If they choose to sell," Kelly said.

"We won't cross bridges till we come to them," Wyman said. "I'm sorry about the mess." He waved at the room. "I must be going now."

"Slight error," Kelly said. "You're not going anywhere. I think Pascal would like to talk to you."

"No!" Wyman said, breathing hard.

"Sorry," Kelly said, "but that's the way it is." He moved away from the door and toward the phone on the bedside table. He saw Wyman's black eyes gauge the distance to the door and he was ready when he made a dash for it. He caught him by the coat collar and yanked him back. "You're staying here, Wyman," he said.

"You can't keep me here," Wyman cried. He swung, wildly, with his right hand, and the diamond ring cut a painful gash in Kelly's cheek. Kelly hit him twice, once in the stomach and once on the point of the jaw as his head came forward. Wyman collapsed.

Kelly, blotting at his cheek with his handkerchief, picked up the phone and called George Rawn's suite...

Pascal pushed his hat to the back of his head and squinted through cigarette smoke at Stanley Wyman. Wyman had managed to get up from the floor, and sat in the room's armchair.

"There's your murderer," Kelly said. He was holding his handkerchief to his bleeding cheek.

"My, my, candidate number three," Pascal said. "You have nothing on 'the shifting sands of time,' Mr. Cotter."

"Look at my room," Kelly said. "It's been searched just as the old man's room was searched after he'd been killed. It's simple enough, Pascal. Wyman murdered George to get those diamonds. He searched George's room to find them, but he failed. Now he thinks maybe George hid them in here. The thing's as good as a confession."

"Not quite," Pascal said. "But it will do until a confession comes along."

"That's ridiculous, Lieutenant!" Wyman said. "It's just that I couldn't wait for police routines. I have to find those stones! I have buyers for them. I've promised to deliver."

"Look," Kelly said. "You're not out a penny on this deal, Wyman. Yo'u've already made a profit. Why can't you buy diamonds somewhere else to satisfy your clients?"

"You don't understand," Wyman said.

"No," Kelly said. "I don't understand. Why must you have these particular stones? You don't even know what they are, beyond the general specifications. Why did you have to kill George to get them? Why did you risk being caught here? What's so special about that shipment, Wyman?"

"N-nothing," Wyman said. "It's just that there's no place I can buy such a shipment at this time. Other importers have already made deals for their goods. I've got to have this shipment to meet my commitments."

"You know," Pascal said. "I don't think you're telling the truth, Mr. Wyman. There *is* something special about that shipment. If there wasn't, why did Jan Spivak offer such a high price for it? Why was Rawn murdered for it? And why have you run such risks to find it?"

Wyman straightened up in the chair, a little spasm of pain twisting his face. "There was nothing special about it, Lieutenant. It was just that it was available."

"It was *not* available, because George had bought it," Kelly said. "Still, you had to have it—you had to murder George in an effort to get it."

"No! No! NO!" Wyman cried.

Kelly turned to Pascal: "If you'd just step out for a short beer, Pascal, I think I could get this monkey to talk!"

Pascal ignored Kelly's suggestion. "I'm going to lay it on the line for you, Wyman," he said. "George Rawn was murdered and his suite searched by the murderer— all to gain possession of that shipment. Now we find you searching Mr. Cotter's room. Any grand jury would put two and two together and come up with an indictment for murder against you. I know you have no alibi for the time. I've checked. I've checked everyone connected with this case whom I could find. If I were the district attorney I'd be pretty certain I could send you to the chair. That being the case, if I were in your shoes I think I'd decide this was no time for secrecy. I think I'd come clean—*if* I was innocent. Because it's an unfortunate fact that innocent people do sometimes burn, Mr. Wyman. Now, what is so special about that shipment?"

"N-nothing," Wyman muttered. "N-nothing special. It's just that—"

"As a matter of fact, I do have some phone calls to make," Pascal said to Kelly. "If I leave you here with Mr. Wyman, and he should happen to talk, you'll give me a full report, Mr. Cotter?"

"You bet," Kelly said, his eyes brightening.

"Wait!" Wyman said. "Listen, Lieutenant; if I tell you what I know about this shipment, will you—will you keep the story private if you're satisfied I haven't killed anyone?"

"I can't promise," Pascal said.

Wyman looked at Kelly, and a little trickle of sweat ran down his cheek. "I'll tell you what I know," he said. "Unfortunately, it places me in a somewhat unethical light."

"Murder is a little more than 'unethical,' " Pascal said.

"I don't know anything about the murder!" Wyman said. "But the shipment—well, there *is* something about that."

"Go ahead," Pascal said.

"It's simple," Wyman said. "When I was dropped from the Syndicate List, Lieutenant, I was left in an unfortunate position. I had funds in England—nearly two hundred thousand American dollars. They won't let you bring money out of England. I was unconcerned, because as long as I was doing business with the Syndicate I could use that money in my dealings with them. But when I was dropped—" He waved his hands.

"You were rich, but you couldn't get at your money," Pascal said.

Wyman nodded. "I had to figure out a way to get a part of it here. I thought of a way. I had had dealings with one of the employees of the Syndicate. I—er—it was those dealings that got me in trouble. Anyway, I approached this man. He was willing to help me out—for a substantial bribe. The idea was this: I got Carla to agree that I could buy her shipment when it arrived. Then I bought diamonds on the open market in England. It was touchy, Lieutenant. I bought diamonds, rough diamonds, weighing exactly the same number of carats as Carla's shipment—but of a superior quality. Fancy goods. My man at the Syndicate substituted these for the goods that were supposed to come to Carla."

"Substituted?" Pascal asked.

"Sure. We put the fancy goods in the package for Carla instead of the intended shipment."

"And what happened to the intended shipment?"

Wyman spread his hands. "We sold it in England— through channels. But no one got cheated, Lieutenant! The Syndicate got *its* money! Carla got her money! All that happened is that I got a hundred thousand of my capital—less expenses—into this country."

"By flimflamming the British Government," Pascal said. "However, that's not my problem at the moment. Those fancy goods of yours still had to get through the U.S. Customs, Wyman. How did you manage it?"

"That was the beauty of the plan," Wyman said. "You see, the customs man would only check to see that they *were* rough stones, and that they *did* weigh the number of carats specified in the shipment. Unless he was an expert, he wouldn't detect the fact that these goods were worth *twice as much* as the shipment intended for Carla. Do you see? It would have been the worst kind of bad luck if the customs man found anything wrong. He didn't, of course, because the shipment came through."

"I still don't get it," Kelly said.

"It had been arranged that I was to buy that shipment from Carla for a hundred and ten thousand dollars. She would have given me time—until I could dispose of them. Actually the shipment was worth twice that!"

"It was a way to get, roughly, a hundred thousand of your capital into this country, as you said," Pascal observed.

"Precisely," Wyman said. "Naturally, Carla didn't know this. She thought she was doing me a favor when she sold to Mr. Rawn making me a ten per cent profit. Actually, that deal cost me ninety thousand dollars instead of making me a profit! You can see now why I *have* to find the shipment."

"Ninety thousand dollars sounds like a perfect motive for murder, to me," Kelly said.

"No!" Wyman cried, waving his hands. "I just wanted the goods."

The telephone on the bedside table rang. Kelly glanced at Pascal, who indicated that he should answer it. He walked over and picked up the receiver. "Hello."

"Kelly?" It was Carla's voice. Kelly felt a pleasant acceleration of his heartbeats. She had used his first name so casually.

"Hi," he said. "This is a pleasant surprise."

"Listen, Kelly," she said. "I'm in a kind of a jam. I tried to reach Lieutenant Pascal but he doesn't seem to be in Mr. Rawn's suite and nobody knows where he is."

"He's right here," Kelly said. "Do you want to talk to him?"

"No time," she said. Her voice sounded low and tense. "I'm alone here at the office. Eddie Mostil's out on an errand. The buzzer just sounded, and I looked out through the panel in the steel door. It's Spivak, Kelly."

"Spivak!"

"I can't let him go," Carla said. "We might not find him again. But I'm a little afraid, Kelly. If he's the one—"

"Listen," Kelly said. "We'll leave here at once. You let him in. Keep him talking. Agree to anything he suggests. Just stall. We should be there in fifteen minutes. Understand?"

"Yes, Kelly."

"Just don't cross him. Let him have his way. But keep him talking!"

"Right," she said. Then her voice faltered: "There's the buzzer again. I'd better—"

"Let him in," Kelly said. "We'll see you—but fast!" . . .

Even police cars with right of way and sirens to enforce it have difficulty with midtown traffic on a rainy afternoon in New York. Pascal and Kelly, with Wyman between them, took up the rear seat of the car. The driver kept his siren wailing, but they moved slowly. Kelly jittered. Pascal went on calmly questioning Wyman.

"Who is Spivak?" he asked for the tenth time.

"I keep telling you, I don't know!" Wyman said.

"Is he, by any chance, your accomplice from London, trying to outbid you for the shipment?"

"My friend's name isn't Spivak!" Wyman said.

"What's in a name?" Pascal said. "Is your friend

about six and a half feet tall, bald as an egg, and—"

"Zabriskie is short and fat," Wyman said.

"So his name is Zabriskie?"

"Yes, yes."

"Perhaps Spivak is his agent."

"I don't *know!*" Wyman said. "I just don't *know!*"

"We could get these last few blocks faster on foot," Kelly said.

"Take it easy," Pascal said. "This Spivak must know the real value of the shipment or he wouldn't have offered such a high price. How could he know, Wyman?"

"I don't know."

"There's only one way. Your friend, Zabriskie, is double-crossing you."

"Please—I keep telling you!" Wyman cried.

Kelly opened the door of the car. "I'm taking it on foot from here," he said.

Pascal sighed. "Okay, if you insist," he said. He spoke to the driver: "Get parked somewhere and come to Room 2209. I may need you."

Kelly ran interference for Pascal and Wyman along the sidewalk. They got into a waiting elevator in the building lobby. Pascal showed his badge to the operator. "Never mind waiting for signals," he said. "Go straight to twenty-two."

The car shot up with stomach-turning velocity. Kelly was first out into the hallway at the twenty-second floor. He ran down the corridor to 2209. The outside door to the waiting-room was open. There was no one in the waiting-room.

The steel door to the inner offices was open. Kelly went through it. Eddie Mostil's office was empty.

The door to Carla's private office was open. But this room, too, was empty—achingly empty because it seemed so neat; the delicate scales under their glass cover, the neat black-baize top to Carla's table, the loupe, the gleaming pads of diamond paper. The chair behind the table, Carla's chair, was pushed slightly back. The chair in which the customer was invited to sit was in place. There was one cigarette stub in the silver ash tray—a Turkish cigarette with a hollow tube mouthpiece. It must have been Spivak's, Kelly thought.

"Carla!" he called out, with the sinking feeling that it was useless.

The safe was closed. The whole place looked as though it had been left for the day—everything except the three open doors, through which Carla and Spivak must have gone.

Pascal stood very still, looking around the office.

"They're not here!" Wyman shouted. "Carla would never go out of the office and leave that steel door open. It would violate her insurance!"

"For God's sake shut up!" Kelly said. He wheeled on Pascal: "Well, what are you going to do?"

"Any suggestions?" Pascal asked, fumbling in his pocket for a cigarette.

Then, from the outer office, they heard a high, offkey whistle. It ended abruptly. "Carla!" a voice called. It was Eddie Mostil, Carla's assistant. He came quickly through his own office and found them standing there. "What cooks?" he asked. "Where's Carla?"

"That's the jack-pot question, son," Pascal said.

"She phoned us Spivak was here," Kelly said. "We told her to let him in and hold him till we got here. We just arrived, and found the place like this—doors open, no one here."

"Spivak!" Eddie said, in his squeaking voice. "There's something fishy going on here, Inspector."

"You're telling me," Pascal said. "And it's 'Lieutenant.' "

"I don't mean just this," Eddie said. "About an hour ago we got a phone call. Some guy who said he was staying at the Vanderbilt Hotel—gave his name as Adams—John Quincy Adams, the Fourth. He said he was in the market for some speculatives. He wanted to see what Carla had to offer. She gave me some stuff to take down to the hotel." He fumbled inside his coat, pulled out a wallet, and removed half a dozen stones wrapped in diamond paper. "You saw some of these the first day you were in here, Mr. Cotter. Well, I took them to the hotel, but there wasn't any John Quincy Adams, Fourth, registered there. So I came back."

"Carla said you were out on an errand," Kelly said.

"It looks more like it was a dodge to get me out of here," Eddie said. "It was probably Spivak all the time! What's he done with her, Inspector?"

"Lieutenant," Pascal said, as though his title was the most important thing in the world. Then, his eyes brightened as they heard footsteps in the outer office. The driver of the police car joined them.

"What did you do, Murphy, park in the Bronx?" Pascal asked.

"There's some excitement downstairs," Murphy said. "Somebody fell down the freight elevator shaft."

Kelly felt his breath catch in his throat. "A woman?" he asked, and didn't recognize his own voice.

"No," Murphy said. "I wouldn't have hung around, Lieutenant, only they'd dug out the guy's papers and identified him, and I heard them mention a name which you were talking about coming uptown: Jan Spivak!"

"Is he dead?" Pascal asked.

"Hamburger," Murphy said casually. "He must of

fell from high up. Wasn't much left of him when he landed in the basement."

"Well, damn it, don't just stand there!" Kelly said. "Spivak took Carla out of here. What did he do with her?"

"Keep your shirt on, sonny," Pascal said. "He can't have taken her very far if he only got to the freight elevator shaft himself." He gave orders to Murphy: This floor of the building was to be searched. The whole building was to be surrounded and searched from top to bottom.

"That'll take a month!" Kelly fumed.

"So it will take a month," Pascal said mildly. Then he turned on Eddie Mostil, and the mildness was suddenly gone: "How do I know your story is true?" he demanded. "How do I know there ever was a John Quincy Adams, Fourth?"

Eddie winced. "There wasn't!" he said. "That's what I told you. But Carla talked to someone on the phone who *said* that was who he was. She sent me with the diamonds. Ask her!"

"I'd like to," Pascal said. "In fact, I'd give a week's pay if I could ask her right now." . . .

At the end of four hours Kelly's nerves were unendurably frayed, and even Pascal looked a little worn and hollow-eyed. The building had been given a thorough going-over. Every out-of-the-way broom closet and storage place had been examined. Every office force in the building had been questioned. The net result was zero.

Now people had swarmed out for the night. Only the building's skeleton staff, the charwomen, a few late office workers, and the little group in the office of Hendrik Van Rooten, Ltd., remained. That group consisted of Pascal, Kelly, and members of Pascal's staff who kept coming in and going out. Eddie Mostil had gone out to get them some coffee and sandwiches. Wyman had been placed under arrest on a technical charge and lodged in the city jail.

There was only one conclusion to draw, and Pascal drew it. "She isn't in the building," he said, "dead or alive. Spivak didn't take her out of the building. He never left it himself. I don't think he fell; I think he was pushed. Unless she left under her own steam and is staying under cover for her own reasons—"

"That's crazy," Kelly interrupted.

"—then there is someone else involved in this. Someone who murdered George Rawn *and* Spivak and who is responsible for Carla's absence. It's not Wyman. Wyman was with us when this second phase developed."

"How about Eddie?" Kelly asked.

Pascal pulled his notes in front of him. He was sitting in Carla's chair behind the black baize table.

"Edward Mostil," he said. "604 East 39th Street. He earns eighty dollars a week. He's grown up in the firm from office boy to Carla's assistant. He was out on an errand when Spivak arrived here. That we have from Carla, and it supports the John Quincy Adams story to some extent. Now get this, Kelly:

"He wasn't here when Spivak arrived. We got here exactly fourteen minutes after Carla's call. If Eddie came in instantly on Spivak's heels, he had a number of things to do in a very short while. He had to break up the conference between Spivak and Carla. He had to get them both out of this office. He had to push Spivak down the elevator shaft, keeping Carla under cover while he did it. He then had to dispose of Carla by hiding her somewhere, or killing her and hiding the body somewhere. And he had to walk back into this office, clean and unruffled, in approximately sixteen minutes! He got here right after us. Figure out how he could manage it, Kelly."

"It doesn't sound possible," Kelly admitted. "But that leaves us looking for someone we don't know about."

"There are two people I'm interested in," Pascal said, "and I'm going to start digging on them now. One is Wyman's friend in the Syndicate office in London—Zabriskie. He knew the real value of that shipment and might go berserk to get it. The other is the customhouse man who passed on the shipment. There'd be nothing illegal in his passing the shipment. It weighed the specified number of carats. There was no question of duty involved. But if he had an eye for stones he, too, knows the real value of that shipment, and he might have interested himself. Those are long shots, but we've got to play them. If we were lucky enough to find that Zabriskie isn't, in fact, in London—that he's here—"

Pascal shook his head. "If that happened, my belief in Santa Claus would be revived."

But two hours later there was no sign of Carla, and Pascal's belief in Santa Claus was right back where it started. A transatlantic call to London developed the fact that Zabriskie was there. The Syndicate official to whom Pascal talked was grateful for the information that Zabriskie had pulled a fast one, but this didn't advance Pascal's case.

The customs people, after a diligent search of the records, were able to inform the Lieutenant that the inspector who had passed on the Van Rooten shipment was one Paul C. Hubbell. Pascal derived a glimmer of hope when he heard that Hubbell was on his annual vacation with his family at Mountain Lakes, New Jersey. But a call to the resort found Mr. Hubbell, angry at being awakened in the middle of the night, claiming he had been with his family all day—a fact which Pascal decided to check, but which he was gloomily certain *would* check.

That was that. Stone wall. . . .

It was hot and humid. It was four o'clock in the morning. Despite the fact that he was close to nervous exhaustion, Kelly Cotter couldn't sleep. He lay on his bed in his room at the Bransfield, eyes wide open, staring at the ceiling. He had been trying for an hour to tell himself that Carla didn't mean anything to him, that she was just a human being in trouble. But her impact on him had been deeper than that, and there was no use kidding about it.

Kelly knew in his heart that Pascal, for all his leisurely approach to the problem, was an extremely thorough police officer. He knew that everything humanly possible was being done. He knew that every cop in New York was alerted, and that a five-state alarm had been sent out.

But why had Carla been abducted—or killed? You had to face that possibility. She, like Spivak, might be lying dead somewhere. But why? She didn't have the diamonds. Was it possible that Spivak, himself, had disposed of her in some way and that his fall had been accidental? That actually they had their murderer, dead, in the morgue? Where could Spivak have hidden Carla? It would have to be somewhere in the office building; there hadn't been time for him to get her somewhere else. And why would he have come back to the building? But Carla *wasn't* in the building. Pascal's men, experts at that kind of search, were certain of that.

Round and round, over and over, the facts ran and turned in Kelly's mind. He went back to the very beginning, to his first visit with old George to Carla's office; to their return to the hotel with the diamonds; to the two hours in which old George had, according to him, hidden the diamonds where "not even the rats in this joint" could find them; to dinner; to their return and the telephone call which old George had taken. That's where things began to go haywire. Old George said Carla was coming. Carla insisted she'd never phoned.

Kelly switched on the bedside light, went over to the bureau, and took out a folded copy of the statement he'd made. He reread that part of it, slowly:

" 'Hello . . . Yes, this is George Rawn . . . Oh, hello! Sure—sure . . . No, I'm still savoring.' And he chuckled. 'Of course. When? . . . Tonight? Well, why not? Be a great pleasure . . . Sure; I'll be here.' And he hung up the phone. 'Tha Van Rooten girl wants to see me,' he said. 'Now. She'll be here in ten minutes.' "

Kelly's eyes, red-rimmed and hot, read the words over again. Certainly old George had been talking to someone he knew. If it wasn't Carla, it had to be Spivak or—or Eddie Mostil. They were the only people, outside of Carla, who knew about the deal. If it was Spivak, pretending to make an appointment for Carla, wouldn't old George have asked him how come? Wouldn't he have been suspicious? But if it had been Eddie, Carla's assistant, George might have assumed it was quite natural for him to call. He'd certainly known the caller; his words, his tone of voice had proved that. Nobody thought of asking Eddie whether he'd made the call. If he had made it, though, he'd made it without Carla's knowledge. She'd said over and over again she knew nothing about it. So, if it was Eddie on the phone, he hadn't been on the level.

Kelly felt the hair rising on the back of his neck. Pascal's time schedule had eliminated Eddie—or so it seemed. But if Eddie had made that call—and the more Kelly restudied the statement, the more it seemed to him it must have been Eddie—then Eddie was involved in this up to his neck.

Kelly picked up the phone and called Homicide . . . Pascal wasn't there. They didn't know where he was. They wouldn't give Kelly his home phone. They finally agreed to call Pascal and ask him to call Kelly. Ten minutes later they reported back. Pascal wasn't home. His wife didn't know where he was.

Kelly took out the telephone book. Eddie Mostil had no listed phone. Then Kelly remembered Pascal's methodical analysis of Eddie's place in the picture. "Edward Mostil, 604 East 39th Street—" He remembered the address clearly. Kelly began getting back into his clothes. This idea about Eddie was steaming-hot. It couldn't wait for Pascal. If Eddie was involved he knew where Carla was. She had been missing now for nearly fifteen hours in God knows what kind of situation. You couldn't let it ride for five minutes if there was any chance of prying her whereabouts out of Eddie.

It didn't take too long at that time of the morning to get uptown in a taxi. It was almost daylight when Kelly got out of the cab opposite 604 on 39th Street. He had no plan, except to somehow pry out of Eddie what he knew.

The building was brownstone, bleak-looking in the gray dawn light. Kelly walked across the street and into the vestibule. Eddie Mostil's name was in one of the brass-framed name plates. Kelly put his finger on the bell and held it there. Almost at once a voice came through the house communicator: "Who is it? What do you want?"

"Eddie? Is that you?" Kelly shouted into the speaker.

"*Who is it?*" Eddie's squeaking voice insisted over the communicator.

"It's Kelly Cotter."

"Oh!" Instantly there was a clicking of the door latch, and Kelly turned the knob and stepped in. The stair well was dimly lit. On the third floor there was an extra glow of light, and looking up, Kelly saw Eddie, his straw-colored hair illuminated by the glow, peering down at him.

Kelly climbed the stairs to where Eddie waited. Eddie had on a bathrobe, but Kelly saw that under it were shirt and trousers. If Eddie had been sleeping he hadn't gone through the formality of undressing.

"Come in, Mr. Cotter," Eddie said, keeping his voice low, apparently in deference to other tenants who were sleeping.

Kelly stepped into a tiny-one room apartment. It wasn't a cheery place. There was a day bed, with a worn bedspread covering it. The spread was wrinkled, as if Eddie had been lying on it, and the ash tray on the little side table was spilling over with butts. There was a worn leather armchair with sagging springs; a battered, Grand Rapids bureau; a bridge lamp, its green shade torn; some books on the bureau-top, all on the subject of diamonds; and newspapers, dozens of newspapers, scattered on the floor around the chair and beside the bed. The bridge lamp was lighted, because it was still dark inside the apartment.

"Has anything happened?" Eddie asked, as he closed the door. "Why didn't you phone me? Have they found Carla?"

"No," Kelly said. Then, for the first time, he noticed the picture of Carla over the bureau. It had been cut out of a magazine which had evidently done a feature on the glamour girl of the diamond business. In the picture she was wearing the dark harlequin glasses which had so irritated Kelly the first time he saw her.

"Sit down," Eddie said. Kelly sank into the deep leather chair. Eddie perched himself on the edge of the bed.

"No, they haven't found Carla," Kelly said. "That's why I'm here, Eddie."

"Gee, if there's anything I can do," Eddie said. "I've known her ever since I was a kid in short pants, running errands for her old man. I'd do anything for Carla."

"Then why don't you tell us where she is?" Kelly asked, very quietly.

"Holy smoke, Mr. Cotter, if I knew—!"

"I just figured things out, Eddie," Kelly said. "It was you who phoned Old Man Rawn the night he was murdered."

"Look, Mr. Cotter; you got it all wrong. I—"

"You phoned him, Eddie, and told him Carla wanted to see him. That wasn't true. It was you who wanted to see him and you who came to the Bransfield. Unless you have an explanation for that phony call, and unless you can prove that it wasn't you who killed the old man and searched his rooms, things are going to be pretty rugged for you, Eddie." Kelly kept his voice conversational.

Eddie lowered his head, and his shoulders hunched in a spasmodic jerk. To Kelly's astonishment, when Eddie lifted his head there were tears in his eyes—tears that spilled over and ran down his cheeks.

"You shouldn't have come here, Mr. Cotter," he said. "I got nothing against you. Nothing at all."

Then Kelly saw the gun. Eddie had taken it out of the pocket of his dressing gown.

"So it was you, Eddie," Kelly said. He sat so still it hurt.

"I never used this," Eddie said, looking down at the gun. "I—I guess it makes an awful lot of noise."

The leather chair was low. To get up from it quickly would require the use of both hands and enough effort to give Eddie much too much time to squeeze the trigger.

"It's crazy," Eddie said, in a choking voice. "It's like a snowball! It keeps getting bigger and bigger. I never meant to kill the old man. I didn't think I had till I heard the next morning he was dead. I just meant to knock him out while I searched the place. Now there's him dead, and Spivak dead—"

"You killed Spivak?" Kelly asked, struggling to keep his tone casual.

"No. But I was in on it," Eddie said.

"Tell me where Carla is," Kelly said. "The game's over, Eddie. It can only come out one place, no matter how much farther you go."

"Not if we had the diamonds," Eddie said. "Not if we had the diamonds, Mr. Cotter. We'd go somewhere—somewhere they can't extradite you. We'd have money. It wouldn't come out bad then."

"We?" Kelly said.

"Sure," Eddie said. "That's why I thought I was safe. Because the lieutenant figured out I couldn't have done it—that there wasn't time. But there was *him*, of course. He killed Spivak and took Carla away."

"Who is 'he,' Eddie?"

Eddie looked surprised. "I thought you'd figured that," he said. "It's Hubbell, the customs man, of course. You got to understand this, Mr. Cotter."

"Yes, Eddie. I'd like to understand it," Kelly said. There was something crazy about the weeping little man with the gun. Time—anything that would make for time—might create a moment when the balance lay another way.

"You wouldn't understand what it's like to always

want something—to always have it right under your hands—and not be able to touch it," Eddie said.

"What did you want, Eddie?"

"Carla!" Eddie whispered. "I'd see her every day—the shape of her, the sound of her, the warmth of her. She was a million miles away from me. But right there—right in my hands—was stuff that would close that gap, Mr. Cotter. Diamonds! I had a fortune in diamonds in my hands every day for years. But I couldn't touch it. If anything was missing, the insurance dicks would slap me in jail. But always—always I told myself, some day there'd come a chance."

"When did it come, Eddie?"

"Last week. This Hubbell came to see me. Maybe he was a little like me—fortunes passing through his hands every day, and none of it for him. You know about the shipment. You heard it from Wyman."

"Yes."

"Well, Hubbell spotted it. The goods added up to the proper weight in carats, but he saw they were worth twice as much as they were listed at. He passed them. There wasn't any risk in that. He was only supposed to certify they were rough goods, as advertised, weighing so many carats. But he figured there was something fishy and maybe some dough in it. He took a chance on coming to see me. If I acted honest and upright, maybe he'd come in for a reward. If I wasn't quite so straight, maybe there was a real killing in it." Eddie's voice broke. "I wasn't quite so straight."

Kelly watched the gun. Eddie held it pointed at him, and his hand was uncomfortably shaky. Kelly didn't dare move a finger.

"I figured things pretty fast," Eddie said. "I knew Carla had promised the shipment to Stan Wyman a long time before. I figured Wyman was using her to get his dough into the country. I justified myself by telling myself he was playing a dirty trick on Carla. I'd do anything for Carla."

"Go on, Eddie."

"Hubbell and I had it figured airtight," Eddie said. "No violence, no nothing. We'd wait till Wyman picked up the shipment from Carla, and then we'd go to him and tell him we knew what he was up to."

"You'd blackmail him for the ninety thousand," Kelly said.

"Sure. He could go to jail. He'd be through with Carla. He'd be out of the diamond business forever—every branch of it. We had him cold. But he didn't get the shipment. Mr. Rawn got it—you and Mr. Rawn! I was nearly crazy. We had to get it back somehow, get it to Wyman, who was naturally crazy for it, too, and then hook him. That's why I went to see Mr. Rawn that night."

A muscle rippled along Kelly's jaw. "And slugged him with that silver flower vase when he wouldn't hand over the shipment."

"I offered him a profit," Eddie said. "I didn't want to hurt him. When he wouldn't listen I just hit him with the flower vase—just to keep him quiet while I searched the place. He was alive when I left. I didn't think he was hurt bad. He must have died afterwards—because he was so old!" Eddie shook his head from side to side. "Where did he hide the diamonds?"

"Where did Spivak fit into this?" Kelly asked.

Eddie seemed to draw his mind back from the nightmare of George Rawn's murder. "When the crooked wheel starts turning, everybody gets on for the ride, Mr. Cotter. Stan Wyman bribed this guy Zabriskie in London to substitute the shipment for him. Zabriskie took the bribe, but he had his own angle. He got Spivak to represent him here—to outbid Stan Wyman for the shipment. He figured Wyman couldn't go too high without rousing suspicion, whereas Spivak could act crazy and no one would care. Spivak could bid a hundred and fifty or seventy-five, and they'd still make a good profit. Wyman wouldn't dare go that high. Carla would know there was something fishy."

"But what happened today when Spivak went to see Carla?"

Eddie drew a deep breath. "I had to get out of the office to see Hubbell and figure our next move," he said. "Hubbell made that phony call from John Quincy Adams, Fourth. I went out with the speculatives, supposedly to show this phony Adams. I was waiting for an elevator when Spivak got off an up-car and headed for the office. I was worried. I went back to see what he was up to. When Carla let him in I switched on the office communicator."

Eddie moistened his dry lips. "It turned out Spivak had been at the Bransfield the night before, waiting for a chance to see Old Man Rawn. He saw me go upstairs. Afterwards, when the murder broke, he knew I'd done it and he figured Carla was in on it with me. He demanded she turn over the diamonds. He figured she had them!"

"I see," Kelly said.

"Hubbell was waiting for me in a phone booth in the lobby of the building. He was waiting there in case I got held up I could call him back. I did call him, and told him about Spivak. He came upstairs. I had this gun. We kept it in the office, you understand. Hubbell had a gun, too. He took Carla and Spivak away with him. He must have pushed Spivak down the elevator shaft to get rid of him. Then he took Carla somewhere. I haven't heard from him since. I don't know where—"

"Slight correction as to detail, sir," said a husky

voice from the deep shadows of the room.

Eddie jerked his head around. Kelly, who had been waiting tensely for his chance, made a dive for the gun—without stopping to think about the strange voice from the shadows. He knocked the gun out of Eddie's hand and started to scramble after it.

"No, Mr. Cotter. No!" the husky voice said. "That would be most unwise."

Then it percolated—the sound of that husky voice—the voice of a prize fighter who had been hit too many times on the Adam's apple. Kelly lifted his head and saw a figure in a loose-fitting suit, a shiny bald head, and eyes that seemed to pulsate behind the thick lenses of his spectacles. Spivak! Jan Spivak, whose remains were supposedly lying under a sheet in the morgue!

It was a totally unbelievable moment. Kelly rose slowly to his feet, his eyes fixed on the snub-nosed pistol in Spivak's long fingers. The light from the bridge lamp cast a yellow circle on the floor—on the gun that had fallen from Eddie's hand. And above, it threw light on the lenses of Spivak's glasses as he moved forward, blotting out the magnified pupils of his eyes.

"As you see, sir," Spivak said, "there was a slight miscarriage of plan. Mr. Hubbell, who intended to take care of me, was—shall we say?—taken care of *by* me! It was his intention to take Miss Van Rooten and me down on the freight elevator, so that we would not be noticed. He rang for the elevator. But he was a nervous man, sir. Extremely nervous. Crime was new to him and he did not know how to watch out for himself.

"And so presently I had his gun. And when the elevator came up I told the operator he was wanted on the floor above. I managed to place the toe of my shoe in the crack of the door so that it did not close. And when the elevator went up, I, sir, disposed of Hubbell, and not he of me. And then I threw my wallet and papers of identification down after him. Believe me"—and the corners of his mouth twitched—"Miss Van Rooten came with me, then, unprotesting. She was convinced I meant business. And I do, Mr. Cotter, I do, sir."

"I believe you," Kelly said slowly.

"Where are the diamonds, sir?" Spivak asked.

"I don't know," Kelly said. "That's the truth. I have no idea."

Spivak nodded his shiny bald head. "I am inclined to believe that. So, we three will go somewhere away from here. We will sit down quietly together and analyze the mind of your late friend, Mr. Rawn, until we can guess where he hid them. You, Mr. Cotter, knowing how his mind worked, will finally figure out the answer to the mystery."

"Perhaps he hid them in the hotel," Kelly said. He could feel the sweat running down his back. "The police are not infallible."

"But I, sir—I *am!*" Spivak said. "I searched the hotel. The diamonds are not there. You see"—and his mouth twitched—"I saw our little friend here leave the hotel after he'd visited Mr. Rawn, and he did not have the diamonds. I knew, because he could not have carried them without my seeing. So I went to visit Mr. Rawn. He was just recovering from the blow our little friend here had struck him. He saw me. That was unfortunate, because of course I had to kill him."

"You!" Eddie said, between chattering teeth. "I didn't kill him. I didn't. You heard that, Mr. Cotter? You heard that?"

"I'm afraid it's not going to do you much good, Eddie," Kelly said.

"I admire the clarity of your thinking," Spivak said. "We will go somewhere and think about where Mr.

Rawn hid the diamonds, and when we have guessed, then I—"

"Then you will kill us," Kelly said quietly.

"Correct—in every detail, sir."

"You can't get away with it," Eddie chattered.

"Oh, but I can," Spivak said. "You see, I—Jan Spivak—am dead. When they find you they will assume your friend Hubbell was the murderer, and they will start searching for him. The search may last for many years—because the police are dogged—but they will not find him. And they will not look for me, because I am dead."

It was neat, insanely neat, Kelly thought. He had a ridiculous picture of Pascal as an old man, telling his grandchildren of his one great failure; the case of the man who murdered five people and disappeared from the face of the earth with a fortune in diamonds. It wasn't a comforting fantasy.

"So we will go from here now, to where we will not be interrupted for a long time," Spivak said. "I will ask you both to march down the stairs."

"One thing I'd like to know," Kelly said. "How did you happen to find us here?"

"I followed you from your hotel, sir," Spivak said. "I thought you might be going to the diamonds. Now, march!"

There was nothing else to do. Kelly had shifted to where the light did not blot out those enlarged black eyes. He saw an insanity of purpose there that warned him against the slightest move. There might come a moment later—if it did not all happen too quickly.

He had to help Eddie, whose legs seemed to buckle under him. In the doorway Eddie checked himself, leaning against the jamb for support.

"I think—I—g-going to be sick at my stomach," he muttered. "B-bathroom back there—"

It happened so fast, so very fast, that Kelly had no chance to save him. Little Eddie blundered backward as if to head for the bathroom, but instead he ran straight into the snub-nosed gun in Spivak's hand.

"Mr. Cotter!" he screamed.

Kelly realized then what he was up to. He made a dive, but too late. Spivak's gun exploded three times, straight into Eddie's body. By then Kelly had the tall man's wrist and arm, and broke the arm across his knee like a man breaking kindling. Spivak's cry of pain ended abruptly as Kelly's fist smashed into his mouth, again and again, as he toppled to the floor like a falling tree.

"Eddie!"

Kelly knelt beside the little man. Eddie was doubled up with pain, and the blood spread over his clothes with frightening rapidity.

"You crazy, brave little fool!" Kelly said. "Sit tight, and I'll get a doctor as soon as I've trussed up this lunatic."

"N-no use," Eddie whispered. "I—I figured it all out. I—I couldn't work for Carla any more. She couldn't have trusted me. And they—they'd arrest me for what I did to the old man. So you find her and tell her I'd do anything for her. Tell her that, Mr. Cotter."

"I'll tell her, Eddie. You can count on it," Kelly said.

Eddie closed his eyes. "I—I wish I knew what the old man did with the diamonds," he whispered. Then he began to cough, and it was the end...

Once in the hands of Pascal and his men, Jan Spivak lost all his assurance. His hand was played out and, knowing that, he talked quite freely. The first and most important piece of information was that Carla was being held in an apartment in Brooklyn. Kelly and Pascal went there in a police car to find her. On the way Pascal told Kelly of his own doings.

"We may not be as brilliant as detectives in books," Pascal said, pulling cigarette smoke into his lungs, "but we are nothing if not thorough. This fellow Hubbell seemed to have an alibi. I'd talked to him on the phone, remember? But I decided to go out to Mountain Lakes and have a talk with him. That's why you couldn't find me when you got your idea about Eddie."

"I thought you were giving me a run-around," Kelly said.

"Just checking, everlastingly checking," Pascal said. "Well, this Hubbell was evidently an amateur, like your friend Eddie. He saw a chance to make a killing and he let his whole family in on it, his wife, his brother, and his sister-in-law. When I called that first time it was his brother who answered the phone. They'd fixed that up in case there were any inquiries while Hubbell was absent from home."

Pascal flipped his cigarette out the car window and promptly lit a fresh one. "The family wasn't hard to break down. They were scared—and the brother, worried about Hubbell's absence, had begun to wonder if Hubbell hadn't run out on them. They talked. I was on my way to pick up Eddie Mostil when we got the report over our car radio that you'd turned in Spivak."

"I hate to think what would have happened if Eddie hadn't decided to turn hero," Kelly said. "Damn it, Pascal, can't this guy drive any faster?"

They found Carla exactly where Spivak had promised. She was trussed up on the bed in the little apartment Spivak had rented for himself, hands and feet held fast by adhesive tape, and a large piece of it plastered across her lovely mouth.

She was a little hysterical when they finally freed her, and she clung to Kelly in a way that made him hope she wouldn't recover too soon. Her story confirmed Spivak's confession. She had seen him get the gun away from Hubbell and calmly push the customs man down the freight elevator shaft. She had realized Spivak was enough off balance so that he wouldn't hesitate to kill her if she made an attempt to get away from him. He had spent hours, when they got to the apartment, in a one-man third degree, trying to get her to tell him where the diamonds were hidden—a piece of information she didn't have.

"I think he would have killed me," she said, "if he hadn't figured out that perhaps he might use me to get Kelly or someone else to talk."

They were in the back seat of the police car, Carla sitting between the two men. Her left hand was tightly entwined in Kelly's right. They hadn't said anything personal to each other, but the feel of her fingers in his told Kelly that he was making headway.

"But where *are* the diamonds?" Kelly heard her ask Pascal.

"Spivak had a good idea, you know," Pascal said. "He was going to sit down with you, Cotter, and get you to analyze the old man's mind. It just happened I've been going through that process of analysis for forty-eight hours. And I think I've come up with something."

"What?" Kelly and Carla asked in chorus.

"Old George Rawn was kind of a screwball, wouldn't you say, Cotter?"

"Definitely," Kelly said.

"He wouldn't put the diamonds in the hotel safe. It

was too late in the day for him to hire a bank vault. We found nothing like a checkroom key or anything of that sort. So I came to the conclusion that maybe he hadn't done any of the usual things we might think of."

"What, then?" Kelly asked.

"We'll see if I'm right, in a moment," Pascal said. "We're just getting there."

For the first time Kelly looked out of the car window to see where they were. It was unfamiliar ground. "Where are we going?" he asked Pascal.

"To a cemetery," Pascal said.

"Cemetery!"

"I told you we check everything," Pascal said. "I checked the old man's story of Dolly O'Connor. I found there was a death certificate recorded in New York and a certificate of burial here in Brooklyn."

"Dolly O'Connor is buried here?" Kelly said. He saw the big iron gates of a cemetery looming before them.

"And I've got a hunch about it," Pascal said, nodding. "You said in your statement that the old man did it up brown. He did. He built a mausoleum—a vault—for Dolly."

Evidently they were expected. At the gate an attendant got on the running board of the car and directed them to the last resting place of Dolly O'Connor, the only woman old George Rawn had ever loved; a huge marble tomb—a little door entering into the earth. The attendant unlocked and opened the door. A marble slab, simply inscribed, set in concrete, covered Dolly's grave. There was a sweet scent of flowers in the place. The flowers were on the floor covering the slab, hundreds of blossoms, all reasonably fresh.

They stood there, looking at the grave, and Pascal

slowly removed his hat, for the first time since Kelly had met him.

"There were two hours that day when you thought the old man was taking a nap, Cotter. I think he came here with these flowers during that time, and I hope—"

He didn't finish, but went over and knelt down beside the flowers. Presently he stood up, and in his hands was the shoe-box-sized package with the heavy customhouse seals intact.

"None of our diamond-hungry friends thought of looking here, because none of them knew George Rawn," Pascal said, his voice oddly gentle. "He promised Dolly diamonds. He was forty years late, but he came through on that promise." He turned the box over and over in his hands—the box which had been responsible for three deaths already, and would add a fourth to its record when Spivak paid for his crime.

"Love is a strange thing," Pascal said. "It happens so fast, and it lasts so long when it's real."

Kelly glanced at Carla, and he saw in her eyes that that was the way she felt about it, too.

Notes
about the
Contributors

"The Empty Hours"   (1960)

To date Ed McBain (Evan Hunter) has published more than 40 novels featuring Steve Carella, Meyer Meyer, and the other detectives of the 87th Precinct. This series, which began in 1956 with *Cop Hater* and which continues to the present—the latest title is *Eight Black Horses* (1985)—has been widely and justly acclaimed as the finest police procedural series ever written by an American. McBain's research into actual police methods is meticulous, up-to-date, and vividly incorporated into his stories; and his understanding of the "cop mind" is acute, as "The Empty Hours" amply demonstrates. Mc-Bain is also the author of another popular detective series, this one concerning Florida lawyer Matthew Hope; the titles, and plots, of each Hope book stem from a different nursery rhyme—*Goldilocks* (1978), *Beauty and the Beast* (1982), *Jack and the Beanstalk* (1984), among others. Under his own name, Hunter is the author of such bestselling mainstream novels as *The Blackboard Jungle* (1954), *Strangers When We Meet* (1958), *Last Summer* (1968), and *Lizzie* (1984).

"Murder in the Dark"   (1949)

In a remarkable literary career that has spanned some sixty years, Hugh Pentecost (Judson Philips) has published more than 100 novels and several hundred short stories. He began writing for the pulp magazines in the 1920s, and published his first novel, *Red War* (a collaboration with Thomas M. Johnson), in 1936. His first book as by Pentecost, *Cancelled in Red* (1939), a mystery puzzle with a stamp-collecting motif, won a Dodd, Mead "Red Badge" prize. Over his long career he has created dozens of series detectives, amateur and professional— among them the hero of "Murder in the Dark," Lieutenant Pascal of New York's Homicide Department. Pascal's other recorded cases have been all too few: he appears in but one novel, *Only the Rich Die Young* (1964), and in two other novellas collected in *Lieutenant Pascal's Tastes in Homicide* (1954).

"Storm in the Channel"   (1944)

Inspector Maigret of the Paris police is, in the words of Ellery Queen, "patient, persevering, painstaking; a bulldog in tenacity, a bloodhound on the hunt with his pipe puffing incessantly, with his placid exterior concealing a shrewd, observant, and highly intelligent brain; often surly as a bear (or as the Seine itself), often peevish and resentful, perplexed and irritable and grumbling, with a heart as big as Paris herself." No more accurate description has been written. Georges Simenon, like his most famous creation, is also a complex and Gallic figure—a phenomenon who has published well over two hundred novels, collections, and nonfiction works over the past fifty years, a large percentage of them featuring Maigret. (The first Maigret novel, *The Strange Case of Peter the Lett*, appeared in 1933; more than 75 titles have followed.) He has led a controversial life, as his recent autobiography, *Intimate Memoirs* (1984), vividly details; but there can be no argument that he is a consummate craftsman in the art of fiction in general and the detective story in particular.

"The Sound of Murder"   (1960)

Donald E. Westlake wears any number of literary hats, all of which seem to fit him perfectly. Under his own name, he has written crime novels (mostly of the comic type), mainstream novels, nonfiction, and numerous short stories. In 1968 he received a much-deserved Mystery Writers of America Best Novel Edgar for *God Save the Mark*, a comedy whodunit with barely restrained elements of slapstick—a type of book no one in the world does better than Westlake. Under the pseudonym of Richard Stark, he is the creator of one of the toughest of anti-heroes, the professional thief known as Parker. Under the pseudonym of Tucker Coe, he is the author of five excellent psychological detective novels about a disgraced New York policeman named Mitchell Tobin. Of his short fiction, "The Sound of Murder" represents one of six stories featuring Detective Abraham Levine of Brooklyn's Forty-Third Precinct, an unusual and highly sympathetic policeman. All six can be found in the 1984 collection, *Levine*.